Simon Raven was born in Charterhouse and King's Co Classics. Afterwards he served Infantry. In 1957 he resigned and turned to book reviewing. His first novel, *The Feathers of Death*, brought instant recognition and his popular *First-Born of Egypt* series encompasses seven volumes. His TV and radio plays, of which *Royal Foundation* is the best known, are classics. He also wrote the scripts for the *Pallisers* series and *Edward and Mrs Simpson*.

SIMON RAVEN

Close of Play

HOUSE OF
STRATUS

This edition published in 2001 by House of Stratus, an imprint of
Stratus Holdings plc, 24c Old Burlington Street, London, W1X 1RL, UK.

www.houseofstratus.com

Typeset, printed and bound by House of Stratus.

A catalogue record for this book is available from the British Library.

ISBN 1-84232-178-1

PART ONE

Beginning of Season

I

A week or so after the crocuses appeared, the Junior Dean gave a party, as he always did, to celebrate the arrival of Spring. He invited all the most clever and amusing undergraduates, and even some who were neither clever nor amusing but whom he felt to need cheering up. He ordered cold food from the college kitchens and the ingredients for a strong but wholesome punch; he looked out his favourite records from the twenties and thirties; and then, almost as an afterthought, he sent further invitations to the ten prettiest girls in Newnham and Girton – enough to be decorative, few enough to give rise to competition and tension, both of which would increase the therapeutic value of the occasion.

One undergraduate whom he nearly did not invite but finally did was called Hugo Warren. For although Hugo was on the whole amusing enough to be asked, the Junior Dean was vexed with him because he had been neglecting his work; and the Junior Dean, while he adored pleasure and was long since emancipated from most kinds of prejudice, was still true enough to his middle-class upbringing to feel that work was important. However, he remembered that Hugo was in some sort a cousin of his old friend, Lionel Escome, and he also remembered that Hugo was leaving that summer and so would not be able to come to the party next spring or any other spring, and in the end he sent him a card. The card arrived only three days before the party, by which time Hugo, thinking he was not to be asked, had decided to do something else; and indeed it would have been a very good thing, in the light of later events, if he had kept to this decision. But it was near the end of the term, money was short, and the Junior Dean's Spring parties were famous in their way; and all these things being so, Hugo changed his mind, changed into his second best suit, and went.

When Hugo arrived at the party, slightly drunk as was his policy, ten men were dancing with the ten prettiest girls from Newnham and Girton, while the rest were drinking the strong but wholesome punch. After Hugo had got himself a generous tumbler of this, he started quizzing the other guests, most of whom he knew; but there was one girl, with fair hair cut like a page boy's, with thin but shapely legs which vibrated while she danced rather as though she were engaged in the act of love, whom he had never seen before. When the Junior Dean asked him to have more punch, Hugo said, "Harold, who is that girl?"

"What girl?"

"The one with the short fair hair and the electric legs."

"She is called Jennifer Stevens," said Harold, "and she is in her first year at Girton."

"How did you find her out?"

"She comes to my lectures."

"Clever Harold."

Harold, annoyed by this patronage, just said, "How is Lionel Escome?"

"Quite well, as far as I know, I shall be seeing him during the vac.," Hugo said, "and I expect he'll come up to play cricket some time next term."

"Good. Give him my love," said Harold, still huffy, and rumbled away with the flowery bedroom jug from which he served the punch.

After this exchange, Hugo went back to admiring Miss Jennifer Stevens' legs. He also drank quite a lot of punch; and by the time Miss Stevens stopped dancing and started, with a healthy appetite and not too much refinement, to crunch a wing of chicken, he had found the courage to accost her. For Hugo was still a very naïf boy, despite his grown-up airs, and he needed stimulus before talking to girls, especially attractive ones, whom he supposed to be the more virtuous in general because they could afford to be particular.

"I'm Hugo Warren," he said, the drink working hard within him, "and I've very much enjoyed looking at your legs."

"Go away, Hugo," said the undergraduate who had fetched Miss Stevens her chicken.

But Miss Stevens was delighted. "Why?" she said.

When Hugo leaned over and whispered in her ear, Miss Stevens went scarlet with pleasure and excitement.

"Bugger off, Hugo, will you?" said the other undergraduate.

"Manners," said Miss Stevens.

Then the gramophone started to play "I've got you under my skin". Without a word, Hugo and Miss Stevens went on to the floor to dance.

"No one's ever spoken to me like that before," she said.

"It's because I'm drunk."

"It was lovely."

Hugo stuck his tongue into her ear and started squeezing one of his thighs against her crutch.

"Oooh," said Miss Stevens. And then, "You must think I'm very silly. But I'm not, you know."

"I'm sure you're not," said Hugo, running a finger along the cleft between her buttocks.

" 'I've got you under *my* skin'," sang Miss Stevens. "Did anyone see you do that?"

"I don't care if they did."

"For God's sake, Hugo," said his host, "stop giving an exhibition at my party."

"There you are, you see," said Miss Stevens.

"Don't be so middle-class, Harold."

"I'm not being middle-class. There's such a thing as overdoing it, that's all."

" 'I've got you under *my* skin'," Miss Stevens sang.

"This young lady and I will now go for a breath of fresh air, which may help us to recover from your gross insults," Hugo said.

"You do that," said the Junior Dean; "and don't take all your clothes off on the front lawn. The porters might look."

"Sauce," Miss Stevens said.

When they got outside, they walked over a bridge and sat down on a bank. Without having been invited, Miss Stevens put her hand inside Hugo's trousers. Since no girl had ever done this to him before, Hugo began to pant with pleasure.

"Go on," she said, "you do it to me too." She guided his hand. "There," she said: "like that."

They played this nice new game with great enjoyment, but in the nature of things it could not last very long.

"Well," said Miss Stevens standing up and getting to work with her hanky, "that was delicious."

"Jennifer," said Hugo, "Jennifer. Sit down again."

"It's damp, it's late, and I'm thirsty."

"Just for two minutes."

"Stop being romantic. If I'd known you were going to be romantic, I'd never have come."

"All right." Hugo stood up and put his arm round her. "When do I see you again?" he said.

"Never, if you're going to be so dreary."

"I can't stay drunk all the time… Tomorrow?"

"I'm going down tomorrow."

"During the vac.?"

"Next term, if I feel like it," she said.

"Why not during the vac.?"

"Daddy's taking me to San Remo."

Hugo did not question this remark. Instead, "What does your father do?" he asked.

"Daddy? Oh, he's just rather rich… Why are you getting so curious?"

"I want to know all about you. Your family, your home…"

"You're just being romantic," she said crossly.

"When next term?"

"When *what* next term?"

"When do we meet?"

"Send a postcard and ask me to dinner. If I'm not doing anything else, I'll come."

By this time they had arrived back at the party. Miss Stevens went off straight away to dance with someone else.

"Harold," said Hugo, "tell me about Jennifer Stevens."

"I've told you. She's at Girton and comes to my lectures."

"No, no, Harold. Tell me who she is, where she comes from…oh, Jennifer."

"I don't know anything more than I've told you already."

"Jennifer," Hugo intoned. "oh, Jennifer."

"For Christ's sake stop being such a c—t," Harold said, "and go away to bed. And don't forget: best wishes to all at Baron's Lodge, when you get there, and love to Lionel."

II

A day or two after all this Hugo Warren went home for the Easter vacation.

On the coast of Kent there are many small harbour towns, the inhabitants of which once got their bread by wrecking, later by fishing and smuggling brandy, but have now been made smugly prosperous by an annual influx of summer visitors. At one of these towns Hugo left the train, walked over the railway bridge, and then struck off along a path which once led over open fields but which now runs, for most of the way, past the villas of shopkeepers and bank-clerks. Yet the path is called Church Straight; and since it does indeed make straight as an arrow for a seemly church, and since along its two mile length there are occasional inns and houses which exhibit the decent proportions of an earlier age, it is still a pleasure to walk up it and to watch the church at its end, which waxes from distant and modest invitation to a genial and almost triumphant welcome of its approaching guest.

"Jennifer," murmured Hugo to himself, and the afternoon quivered with madrigals.

After a time the villas become fewer. At last there is a meadow on either side. Then there is a pub with a bowling lawn, and opposite this a graveyard, overgrown with nettle and bramble, which they took to using when the earth under the church walls was full and which has now, in its own turn, been long disused. Beyond this is yet another pub, named after an admiral who has been dead and obscure these two hundred years but is still honoured here in his birthplace; then there is the church, square and rubicund in authority and welcome; and finally, fronting a road which has come through the orchards from Canterbury, there is a manor house, built now in the style of the early nineteenth century, but which has been in this place, in one shape or another, for close on a thousand years.

"Oh, Jennifer," said Hugo, and all the birds seemed to answer him with their songs of love.

The manor house is called Baron's Lodge, possibly because it was once inhabited by a baron of the Cinque Ports, possibly in reference to an earlier tenant, who held all the land around from his sovereign, Plantagenet, and grew rich from his infamous dealing with mariners unfortunate enough to stray near his coast. However this may be, there are now trees on either side of Baron's Lodge which hide lawns and rose beds and long walls of fruit; and beyond these walls is a wide, green field, carefully tended and planted round with guardian oak and beech. On most days, if you come down the road from Canterbury, you will hear rising from this field the voices of young children; for Baron's Lodge is now a Preparatory School for the Sons of Gentlemen, and it was to the Headmaster and his family that Hugo returned whenever he returned to his "home."

Hugo was an orphan. When he was twelve years old, a pupil at Baron's Lodge, James Escome, who was both his headmaster and a distant cousin, had sent for him one autumn morning and said: "I'm afraid your mother and father have been killed, Hugo. Air-raid in London. Can you think of any relations we ought to let know?"

"No, Uncle James."

"I thought not. And all their friends must be in Japanese prison camps by now. Nothing to be done about them."

"No."

"Well," James Escome had said, briskly but kindly, "your home is here now. I'll see the lawyers and fix it all up. Want to go upstairs for a bit? Spend the day with matron?"

For a moment the enormity of his loss, the ineluctable fact that he could never see again the two people he loved most, had begun to force itself into his consciousness, causing his legs to tremble until he nearly fell. Then he had sensed the dangers and agonies which would lie in facing the truth. Keep away from it, his instinct said, forget it, pretend you never even knew them… Or at least that you didn't care for them much and are rather glad they're dead. Yes, that's it; how nice to be free both of their affection and their demands.

"Well?" said James Escome.

"Thank you very much, Uncle James. And thank you for saying I can live here. If it's all right with you, I think I'll just go back to my form."

"Off you go then," said James Escome, and turned down his eyes.

Now, as Hugo crossed the Canterbury road and walked up the short drive, he saw that James Escome was standing on the steps. He was smoking a pipe and giving anxious little glances down the road, the way a taxi would have come from the station. For a moment Hugo forgot his Jennifer.

"Uncle James," he called, "Uncle James."

"Hugo…" said Escome gently. Then a hearty handshake, a resumption of the usual gruff manner.

"Thought you'd get a taxi. Come out for a breath of air to look for it."

"I left my luggage and walked up Church Straight."

"Quite right. Beautiful day. Now come and have tea. Georgy and Bessie want to see you."

"Lionel?"

"Amusing the children."

A raucous shout rose in confirmation from behind the house, blotting out birdsong. Escome and Hugo went up the steps and turned through a long, low drawing room, at the end of which were open french windows.

"Tea outside on the terrace," said Escome: "celebration." He chuckled. "Celebration of spring, not of you." Very lightly, he squeezed Hugo's elbow. A tall young woman stood up behind the silver tea-table. "Hugo," she said (an echo, almost exact, of Escome's greeting a few minutes before) and kissed him on the lips.

"How are you, Georgy?"

"Busy. Bessie and I are still coping with the end of the mumps. She'll be down in a moment."

Georgiana Escome was James' daughter and a year older than Hugo. She had been educated at Baron's Lodge, among the boys and almost as a boy, until blatant pubescence had rendered this arrangement unsuitable. Hugo still remembered how, a day or two after his parent's death, Georgy had come up to him and said gravely, "I'm very pleased that you're coming to live with us."

Once again the intolerable truth of his loss had threatened to break in on him, although he had now had time to strengthen his defences, to cement and buttress the wall of his indifference. Just for a second, his lip had quivered and his eyes had blinked; and Georgiana, pitying him for the wrong reasons, had seized his hand and held it briefly between her warm, new breasts.

Now she sat pouring out tea, visibly exercising the care that was needed to offset her natural clumsiness.

"Well, Hugo lad?" said a broad voice behind him.

"Hullo, Bessie," he said diffidently. He had always been nervous of this woman. At first James' senior matron, then, after his wife died bearing his daughter, his housekeeper as well, Bessie had now surrendered the keys of the larder to the grown Georgiana but had retained those of the medicine cupboard and the prestige which went with both sets. Hugo remembered, with distaste, how she had heard his prayers when he was little and coolly rebuked him, when he was some years older, for failing to wash properly "underneath there."

"He looks a bit peaked, Mr Escome," Bessie said. "Have they been working you too hard at your books, lad?" The irony was faint but unmistakable. "He'll be in need of feeding up," she went on, "and some good air. The air on those fens carries damp into the soul itself."

"Tea, Bessie?" said Georgiana rather sharply.

"Thank you, love. But I can't stay long. They'll be fretting up there in their beds with the spring just outside the window."

"What news of Cambridge?" asked James.

"Nothing much." His mind was running once more on the dactyllic rhythm of Jennifer's name. They were kind and he loved them, but Bessie's innuendoes stung, and he was irritated even by James, who ought to have known by now that a general request for news was always the most inhibiting, the most crushing question of all.

"Weather was bloody," he said curtly, "till a week ago. Harold gave a party. He sends his best wishes to all of you – and love to Lionel. I'd better go and tell him."

"Surely it can wait – " began Georgy.

"I'll go now."

James turned his eyes down. "You'll find Lionel on the field," he said.

"See you all later," Hugo said, less harshly this time. Oh, Jennifer, Jennifer. And that night you took my hand, and you said...

"Spring," he heard Bessie saying as he walked away along the terrace. "Don't fret, Georgy love. It just makes them restless, that's all."

Lionel and some of the older boys were putting up the cricket nets, while one of the younger masters conducted a yelling and sprawling wide game in the background.

"Bit early?" said Hugo.

"Father wants to give the first eleven a little practice before they go home," Lionel said. "The ground's too dry for rugger now. And you and I can use them in April. What news of Cambridge?"

"The same as ever," said Hugo, suppressing a fresh spurt of irritation. "Harold sends love."

"How is the old thing?"

"All right. I don't think he's very pleased with me, though."

Part of the wide game surged round them and was gone.

"None of these young masters can keep order," remarked Lionel equably. "Why is Harold not pleased with you?"

"He thinks I don't do enough work."

"Is he right?"

"I've done enough to see me into a comfortable second."

"Two-one or two-two?"

"Two-two, unless I'm very lucky. Fair enough, don't you think?"

Lionel walked over to a guy-rope and started to test it. The limp which he had brought back from Normandy showed rather more than usual, as was often the case when he was uneasy or upset.

"We don't want these ropes too tight," he called to his assistants. "They shrink if it rains, and then where are you?"

'Where, sir?" said an assistant.

"Left with a bust rope and your nets on the ground. Good thing to remember if ever you sleep in a tent."

He limped back towards Hugo.

"What you really mean," he said, "is that it doesn't much matter what sort of degree you get because you're only going to teach in a prep. school."

"I didn't say that."

"As a proposition," said Lionel ignoring the interjection, "it is at least partly true. You already *know* enough to teach anything we could possibly want. And as for putting it across, that comes either from experience or instinct. Cambridge can't help much with that."

"Well then?"

"It's a question of attitude, Hugo. You'd have a very good chance of a first if you tried. But because there's no immediate or practical reason for getting one, you settle for what's just good enough to keep you from looking foolish."

"There are other things to be had from Cambridge beside a degree."

"I dare say. If you're keen on acting or politics or writing novels... But all you've done is play a little cricket and sit on your behind."

"What about life, Lionel?"

"People always start talking about 'life'," said Lionel, "when they're busy wasting it. 'Life' is the standard excuse of the second-rate man. 'Ah,' he says, 'I may not have done much but I do know about "life".' On examination, 'life' turns out to be nightclubs or shop-girls or just drifting about – whatever his pet form of self-indulgence may be."

He wandered off to help a small boy who was in trouble with a mallet. Lionel, reflected Hugo, had always taken it upon himself to deliver advice or reprimand. Far more so than James, who would respond to some particular cause of displeasure only with some general remark or gesture, so that the displeasure itself was then generalized and affected one no more than a gloomy broadcast by an Archbishop or the Chancellor of the Exchequer. Typically, it had been Lionel, then nineteen and newly commissioned into the Rifle Brigade, who had given Hugo the traditional moral briefing before he first went to Rugby.

"You'll find," Lionel had said, "that you can get away with almost anything as long as you keep your mouth shut about it. But sooner or later you'll be tempted to open your mouth, and if you don't someone else will. That's the practical reason for being careful. But there are other and better reasons. Perhaps the best word I can use is "self-respect". Your self-respect will soon warn you if you're getting into anything you ought to avoid."

"I don't want to…well…miss anything," Hugo had said. ("Life" again, he supposed as he remembered.)

"You won't miss anything worth having if you do as I say. And another thing. Whatever you're doing do it as well as you can. Not for the prizes and so on, but because it's a waste not to. Anyhow," Lionel had added with a momentary and unexpected air of disillusionment, "the time goes quicker that way."

"Time for the brats to have their tea," said Lionel's voice in his ear. "All in for tea," he called.

"Crace, Dixon, Murray," shouted the young master at the top of his voice, "collect the stumps and the whitewash pail."

Regardless, the mob thundered on.

"Crace, Dixon, Murray," said Lionel, almost to himself.

"Sir?" Three small boys were ranged in front of them, each with his hands behind his back.

"Collect the stumps and the whitewash pail."

"Yes, sir. Now, sir?"

"Yes, sir. Now, sir… These young men will shout so," said Lionel as the boys disappeared. "They ask to be disobeyed." He slipped his arm through Hugo's. "There now," he said, "don't be sulky with me. I'm sorry for lecturing you on your first day home. Come and have a look at the pavilion. I've made a few improvements."

Slowly, they walked across the field. Lionel's limp was still more evident than it should have been. Then he said, "Hugo… You're quite sure you want to start teaching here in September?"

"I think so. Uncle James has always taken it for granted. And so have I."

"Father would be very pleased, Hugo, and so should we all. He'll have to give up soon, then I shall take over, and there's nothing I'd like more eventually than to have you as a partner. But you mustn't come back here just because of us. Or because of anything you think you owe us. After all, your parents left plenty of money to cover all that. And a bit over if you need help to start on something else."

"It's not a question of money, Lionel."

"Nor should you feel bound by any other pressure. It's that sort of thing makes families hate each other so much. Moral blackmail."

"I want to come. I've always thought it a very…decent…way of life. Of course…"

"Of course what?"

Jennifer. Of course Jennifer. Would she remember not to shout at the boys? Or accuse them, in the cool, correct tone, of not washing "underneath there"?

"Nothing, Lionel. Nothing at all… You've certainly put in some work here. These boards…"

There were thirty-five boards on the inside wall of the pavilion, all of them new since he had last been there, each one bearing ten names in red and one in gold.

"I'm glad you like them. They go right back to when father first took over. Of course it isn't much, being in a prep. school cricket XI. But it always seems to me that there should be some visible record of these things. There is usually someone who cares enough to look at them and remember…"

Someone like James or Lionel or Bessie, even someone like Harold or himself. But what would Jennifer answer if one said. "Do you remember how that boy made a hundred one summer afternoon? And caught the winning catch in the last over?" What would Jennifer answer to that?

After dinner James Escome produced some brandy.

"If you'd like to make yourself useful," he said to Hugo, "you can take the Common Entrance candidates for the last ten days of term while I concentrate on the Sixth. Scholarship exams in May. Time running out."

"How does the form book read?"

"No trouble about the C/E people. But some of these aspirant scholars are a bit out of their depth."

"Prospects?"

"Two chaps odds on for the Eton list," said James. "A level money chance at Winchester and a trial runner at Rugby who could be lucky. Possible fake Exhibition at Tonbridge – one of those damn things put up for the sons of bank managers. Any price you like for the rest of the field."

"Not too bad then. Average year?"

"Not quite."

The telephone rang. James listened with controlled irritation to a non-stop harangue in female tones. Every thirty seconds he tried to get a word in but was remorselessly beaten down. Finally he said, very firmly and clearly, heedless of the voice that was still quacking at the other end, "I'm very sorry, Mrs Hunt. I've already discussed this several times with your husband, and you both know very well that it is not possible."

"What did she want, Daddy?" said Georgiana, a faint streak of worry between her eyes.

"Same thing," said James.

"Mumps trouble?" asked Hugo. "Request to pay in instalments?"

"A woman with an obsession," said Bessie. "Tell him, Mr Escome."

"It's a silly story," said James.

"I'd like to hear it."

"Well, there's a draper in the town called Hunt – nice chap who plays golf rather well and has been in a good way of business since the war. A few weeks ago his wife got the idea that it was the smart thing to do to have a boy at a preparatory school. You know, not one of these bucketshop schools, but somewhere – well – *pukkha*, like this place. The Hunts' own son was eleven and a half, and she reckoned it was just the ticket for him to come to us. Upshot was, Hunt collared me one Sunday morning at the golf club and said what about it? So I said we usually liked to get our hands on boys when they were eight or nine, and that in any case all our places were booked up years ahead. No casual vacancies. Whereupon Hunt looked rather relieved, I thought, and said he'd tell his wife."

"But that wasn't the end of it?"

"Oh dear no. Next thing I knew the fellow's wife was up here, with a hat six foot high and her feet bulging out of her shoes like cottage loaves. I told her what I told Hunt, the simple truth, but she just wouldn't listen. Didn't seem to hear – not that she gave me time to say much. So when she'd gone I wrote a note addressed to both of them, repeating in words of one syllable that I could not and would not have their son at Baron's Lodge."

"And they thought you were being snobbish?"

"Exactly. So then I weakened. I was sorry for Hunt, too, because I knew that wife of his must be making his life a misery by now, and I weakened. I said that since this was a local boy, and since his father was an old acquaintance, I would find a vacancy – on one condition: that the boy measured up to a tolerable standard of education. Otherwise, I said, at his age he'd be made thoroughly miserable and be the most frightful nuisance."

"Wise to give way?"

"Not at all. But caught on the flank, you see. Anyhow, Master Hunt came up to be investigated and turned out to know absolutely nothing. He could barely read. Told me he'd come top in plasticine modelling or some bloody nonsense in the school he was at, but as far as I could see he was just sub-cretinous. So I sent him home and I rang up Hunt and I explained, as politely as I could, that the thing was out of the question. Hunt saw my point – sensible chap – and said they'd try somewhere else down the coast."

"How did Mum take it?"

"Ah. Mum, meanwhile, had been going all round the town announcing that little Pee-Wee was off to Baron's Lodge in May. Pee-Wee had become – what's that new expression? – a status symbol. So it was a real slap over the chops when Hunt broke the news. But she's not the kind to give up – I'll say that for her – and no argument can daunt her. Hardly a day passes without her telephoning, and she's even offered to pay fifty per cent more than the normal fee. And that's not the end of the story."

James paused to pour some more brandy into his glass. Georgy went patiently on with her lists. Lionel was looking at an exercise book and Bessie was straddling the fire.

"Other local people had got so sick of Mrs Hunt's boasting that they began to ask if their sons could come here too. Someone even seriously proposed a fifteen-year-old with a moustache – Master Shanks the grocer's son, that was. So I just said that young Hunt was not coming and I hadn't any places anyhow. But the thing had gone too far. Mrs Hunt had been humiliated and needed a way out. She's started a sort of cabal. All the disappointed parents. Accusing us of being arrogant and undemocratic and of reacting against modern trends in education – Mrs Hunt's version of Pee-Wee's failure being that we refused him because he hadn't been taught any Latin."

"But they can't do you any harm. Not with the parents who *matter* to you."

"Georgy thinks they'll try to stir up bad feeling locally," said James airily, "but I tell her they're only small tradesmen and junior civil servants. There's nothing they can do to us."

"What about Granger?" Georgy said.

"The taxi-man who drove us to matches?"

"He's been doing that for twenty years," said Georgy, "even during the war. Now he says he won't do it any more because he's not treated with proper respect at the schools we go to."

"He'll come round," said James. "He's just getting old and tetchy. Granger wouldn't miss one of our cricket matches. You'll see."

"What did Mrs Hunt say just now?" asked Lionel.

"She suggested that if Baron's Lodge was so full up, I might start taking Pee-Wee and his chums as day boys."

"Brass neck," said Bessie.

"She is a ridiculous woman," said Georgy, "but she is quite powerful. She sits on a lot of committees and there's talk of her for councillor."

"Damned interfering bitch," said James. "It's getting as bad as America."

"I think, Daddy, that if we could find some way of quietening her down…"

"Throw a bucket of water over her, that's how you quieten nuisance bitches… Come along, Hugo," said James as he poured himself more brandy; "I'll show you what to do with these Common Entrance candidates."

The next few days passed very pleasantly for Hugo. The Common Entrance candidates were a friendly lot and, as James had said, well up to what would be expected of them. And the fine weather held, so that every afternoon James and Lionel and Hugo could take the older boys for cricket practice at the nets.

"Just the thing," James said: "gets them into the rhythm of the game weeks before anyone else has even thought about buying a bat."

Although James Escome, who had once played for Kent, cherished his cricket elevens with something near passion, he was at the same time entirely liberal about the game. If people weren't interested in cricket, he thought no worse of them and mostly let them play tennis or hunt butterflies instead. If they liked the game and were good at it, they had a lot of fun out of matches both at home and away but were given no special privilege or authority on account of their prowess. At Baron's

Lodge there was no suggestion, as there was at so many schools, that skill at cricket implied moral excellence or that the game itself was a proving ground for life. It was a damned good game if you happened to like it, and that was all. Cricketers at Baron's Lodge gave themselves no airs, were seldom the subjects of jealousy or uncommon remark. In consequence they were pleasant people to spend the afternoons with; and as the hours went by, well ordered and well spent, Hugo began to throw off his fever under their quiet persuasion, so that sometimes a whole day passed during which he never thought of Jennifer at all.

"Who was that woman who *glared* at us?" said Hugo to Georgy as they walked along the sea-front.

"That," said Georgy, "was Mrs Hunt."

"I see what you mean. Formidable."

'Vicious."

"Oh, come, come, dear. Small town hates and all that…"

"Yes," said Georgy, "vicious."

"The general," announced Hugo, "said that the enemy would not conquer the city. Lynch."

"Imperator dixit –"

" – Symmonds."

"Imperator negavit…"

"Good. If there is a negative in the indirect statement, Lynch, we do not normally use *dico* followed by a negative but *nego* followed by an affirmative."

"But sir. The book says you *can* use *dico* with a negative."

"You *can*, Lynch, but it is not customary. And examiners of all people set great store by custom."

"…That was a jolly good story, sir. But I like the one about when you were an officer in Kenya better. That was *super.*"

21

"Don't get rosy ideas about the Army, Symmonds. It's not much fun really," Hugo said.

"Then why were you in it, sir?"

"I had to be. I was doing my period of National Service."

"Did you see any dead men, sir?"

"Several."

"What did they look like?"

"Like life-size dolls," Hugo said. "There's nothing frightening about a dead man, Symmonds. He's just...well, meaningless. All you have to do is get him out of the way as quickly as possible in order to keep the world tidy."

Hugo went to Bessie's room to give her a message from Lionel. She waved him into a chair and gave him a glass of sherry.

"Looking forward to starting next September?" she said.

"Very much, on the whole."

"It won't really be before time," she went on. "The sooner Mr Escome gives up, the better. And when he does, Lionel will need your help."

"Uncle James still seems very spry to me."

"So he may do. Specially when he's got a glass or two in him. But he's over sixty. If he goes on working as he does, on one of these fine and not too distant days he'll just cave in."

"He won't like giving up."

"He won't need to give up altogether. He can still take the odd lesson and help with the cricket. But he can't go on being the big boss much longer. It's time Lionel did that. And time you took your share."

"I'll be glad to."

"And I'm glad to hear you say so," said Bessie. "Sometimes these last days I've thought you had other ideas in your head."

"None that need prevent me coming here."

"Anyway," said Bessie, "you must come."

"Don't nag, Bessie."

"I don't mean to, laddie. Just to let you know that though they don't say much they're putting their trust in you. More trust than you warrant, I dare say. You mustn't let them down."

Hugo set his glass on the table more firmly than was necessary.

"Thanks for the sherry, Bessie. Any answer for Lionel?"

"Just say the boys' trunks will be coming down on Wednesday, so I'd be glad of the gardener's help for a couple of hours. That's all, laddie. And don't forget what I've been telling you."

"Foot, Waddell, *foot.* You must move into the ball and not away from it."

"But, sir, when I was at Canterbury last summer I saw Cowdrey step right away from a fast one so that he could cut it."

"When you've got an England cap you can do the same. Meanwhile we'll stick to first principles. Now. Try it again…"

This time Waddell did as he was told. The ball flew along the netting with a crisp, whirring noise which gave Hugo a curious satisfaction. It seemed to convey achievement and even fulfilment.

"Well done, Waddell," he called; and received in return a beautiful grin of thanks.

And then suddenly all the boys had gone. One evening the corridors were full of scurrying feet and ringing bells, the next morning they were empty, save for two or three morose boys whose parents were late in collecting them. Hugo went up to the field, where he found Lionel quietly weeding the square at its centre.

"I hate weeding," Lionel said, "but I hate meeting parents still more. They ask such fatuous questions – mothers about pants, fathers about marks. As though they were inquiring after Stock Exchange prices."

"Is little Johnny a good investment? Bourgeois attitudes are very perturbing, Lionel, but you'll have to get used to them in this business."

"I'll face up to all that when the time comes. Meanwhile, Bessie and father can cope."

"How very unlike you to evade a responsibility."

"This is my one indulgence," said Lionel. "No parents. They are so patronizing with it all. They seem to think that it is the duty of a schoolmaster to be poor, humble and dedicated, and that this entitles them to treat him either as a species of upper servant or else as someone of good family who has come down in the world and is only noticed out of charity. Those that are late paying what they owe us are the worst."

"They wish to emphasize your unworldly role and indicate that you should not think about money."

"Possibly. And at least their financial predicament gives them some excuse," Lionel said. "But it is as well you should know what you will have to put up with."

He straightened up and lit a cigarette.

"Take the following incident – which is far from untypical. A month ago a man and woman of my own age visited their son here, and I was pressed into showing them round the grounds. I'd met them once or twice before, and on this occasion the woman started addressing me as 'Lionel' – a very dubious familiarity. Still, I thought, let it pass, she means no harm, and by way of return I then called her by her Christian name, which was 'Felicity'. 'This is the gymnasium, Felicity,' I said. She looked at me as if her dog had addressed her in Hebrew. 'I don't think you know me well enough to use that name,' she said. 'Then do you know *me* well enough to call me "Lionel"?' I replied. 'But that,' she said, 'is different.' You see what I mean. She was using my Christian name, as she would that of a footman or a small child, to emphasize the difference between us."

"What did her husband do?"

"Just looked miserable and kept quiet. It's usually the women who make the trouble. They think that because their husbands pay a fee it gives them manorial rights in the place. And that's not all of it. I said just now that the late payers were the worst, but it's not quite true. The very worst are those who plead poverty or special circumstances and persuade us to knock a bit off the bill."

"Are they many?"

"More than you'd think. We always make a reduction if two or more brothers are here, and we often help army officers or clergymen, particularly if the child is supposed to be bright. And what thanks do we get? Complaint and contumely. Once we took a naval chaplain's three boys for only just over the price of one – and the damned fellow came down in a brand new Rover and complained that father had been teaching the Sixth that the book of Genesis was not the whole and literal truth."

"How did Uncle James cope?"

"Told him if he didn't like it he could send his sons somewhere else."

"Did he?"

"Not him. He knew a good thing all right. It was between theology and the Rover, and the Rover won... When are you going back to Cambridge?"

"Just over a fortnight," Hugo said.

"Then we can have a walk or two and a game of golf. And you'll have time for some of your own work now. If you could get a really decent second...or even a first...then..."

"Then what, Lionel?"

"Father and I would be most awfully pleased. For your sake, not ours. Care to help with these weeds?"

"Gladly."

Hugo took off his coat and bent down next to Lionel. Presently Hugo said, "You'll be coming up to Cambridge to play cricket next term?"

"For the Greenjackets against the college. It's my one outing from here between April and August," Lionel said, "and I wouldn't miss it if two bishops and a field-marshal were coming down to visit their brats."

A day or so later Hugo went for a walk with Georgy along the golf course by the sea. The weather still held; the sun was genial but unobtrusive, and a faint, warm breeze raised a delicate piping of foam along the waves. For a long while Georgy remained silent, until Hugo said, "There is no charge for light conversation. What's the matter?"

"Two things," said Georgy precisely.

"Tell."

"This Mrs Hunt, for a start."

"What's she up to? Still alienating the locals?"

"I think so. You see, for years now we've had a system whereby we pay tradesmen a term in arrears. They provide what we need from January to March, say, and we pay them at the end of April with the money which the parents pay us, in advance, as fees for the Summer term. But now two of them have said they want to put an end to that and have their accounts settled monthly."

"Hardly the end of the world?"

"If all the tradesmen do the same, it will make things rather difficult."

"But surely," said Hugo, "there's no shortage of money. The school's well found, every place is taken. Uncle James *must* be running at a profit."

"He should be but he's so casual. He spends a lot of money, on things for the boys, and then doesn't charge the parents. He lets too many in at reduced fees. And he spends quite a lot on himself in a quiet way. Wine for dinner every night – often for the young masters as well. All those clubs of his. Dinner parties he gives, both here and in London."

"So you really *need* next term's fees before you can pay last term's bills?"

"That's it, I'm afraid."

They were among the sand dunes now. Hugo selected a bank for them to sit on, and the sand was warm and welcoming.

"But surely there must be some capital," Hugo said.

"A very little money your parents left which is held in trust for you. All father's is tied up in the school."

"But the bank manager will give you an overdraft if you need ready money. The buildings, the grounds – you've got security for thousands."

"We may have to ask. But if Mrs Hunt can get at tradesmen she can get at bank managers."

"Oh, Georgy, come now – "

"Bank managers aren't perfect. They're often just bitter little men bored with their safe jobs and plain wives and resentful of their social position. They're quite ready to be spiteful if they can find a good excuse."

"But Uncle James knows his man well."

"He's retiring. Sometime in July. God knows who'll come then."

"You worry too much," Hugo said.

"Someone has to. Father can't and Lionel won't."

"Well I'll help you with your worrying from September on."

"You're one of the things I worry about," said Georgy, pulling at the spiky grass. "Two things, I said. You're the second."

"Oh?"

"There's something you want which we can't give you here. I had hoped..."

"Yes?"

"That perhaps I might be able... But I'm not sure... And anyhow you've given no sign."

The sand had warmed his loins and he remembered the childish breasts between which she had once held his hand. He leant over and kissed Georgy, who received him with open lips.

"There." He fumbled at her blouse.

"No, Hugo, no. You must be slow…*kind…*"

"Like this." He guided her hand, just as Jennifer had guided his.

"Oh my God. Hugo – "

"Like this. And then I…"

"Hugo… Do you want to so badly?"

"Yes, yes. Like this." Fiercely he nudged her hand into movement, while she received his without assistance or response.

"That's it, Georgy. Nice. Nice. Is it nice for you too?"

"I don't know. Hugo…I…"

"Don't be so tense, Georgy. Let yourself go."

"I…don't think I can. Hugo, what – "

"Don't talk any more, Georgy. Don't…talk…"

Later on Georgy pulled at her rucked up skirt and avoided his eye. Hugo smoked and fidgeted.

"Time to go home."

"Yes, Hugo. It wasn't any good, was it?"

"It was fine, Georgy, fine." His voice was ungenerous, that of the guest making polite adieux after a badly cooked dinner. A last effort at good manners: "I only wish that you… Do you think…?"

"Not like this. Not suddenly. Not this way."

"There is so much more," he began doubtfully. But he had no heart left to reassure his hostess. After a bad dinner you cut your losses and rang for a taxi at ten sharp. "Come on," he said, "we must go."

Hugo was not once alone with Georgy during what remained of his vacation. This was only a few days, but even these he cut short by saying that he must make up some nights' residence before full term started; and then he left them, Georgy grave, James and Lionel puzzled and hurt, Bessie poker-faced, almost a week earlier than they had expected.

III

"HUGO?"

"Yes, Jennifer?"

"Would you like to try that new thing again?"

"*Yes.*"

In the three weeks of the Summer term which had now passed they had advanced a long way beyond the infantile proceedings of the previous March. While Jennifer had usually taken the initiative, Hugo had cooperated with zeal and fearlessness; so that their mutual enterprise of education had now covered most of the syllabus. There were only, as it were, a few footnotes in small type still to be investigated, and with one of these they were busy this afternoon.

"I think…a little more to the left."

"Like that?"

"Aaah."

At first Jennifer had been unwilling to see Hugo. His postcards were torn up, his invitations unacknowledged. Then he had met her at somebody's party; having contrived to get her by herself, he had not annoyed her by being what she called "romantic" and was inspired by his long absence from her to such feats of improvisation (for once it was Hugo who provided the leadership) that she had been compelled to recognize an immense natural talent. After that they saw each other nearly every day, usually in the afternoons, when Jennifer would sport

Hugo's oak on arrival and go straight through to his bedroom without even saying "Hullo".

"That was super," Jennifer said. "You were terrific."

"So were you...Jennifer?"

"Yes?"

"Why do you never let me kiss you on the lips?"

"No fun in it. Not to me."

"But it is a sign," said Hugo, "of affection and tenderness. I like to give such signs."

"You'll be talking about *love* next."

"And why not?" He raised himself on his elbow. "Why shouldn't I talk about love? Does it never strike you that we are both much too mechanical, much too cold-blooded, about all this? Just using each other's bodies... We hardly ever talk of anything except *this*. Never of our homes or our futures, our interests, our work..."

"How do you know I've got any?" Jennifer said.

"I sometimes wonder. Jennifer. Today, just for once, just for a little while, we must do something different. Will you come for a walk with me?"

"Where to?"

"Fenner's."

"Fenner's?"

"You know, the University cricket ground."

"Christ almighty," Jennifer said.

"Well, at least you'll come out to dinner?"

"A girl must eat," said Jennifer, "but there's hours before we need think of that."

And she started tracing a slow line from the point of his chin and down towards his navel.

"Jennifer," said Hugo firmly, pouring her a glass of wine, "what is to happen later?"

"Later?"

"When I leave Cambridge. Which is in June."

30

"What should happen? You go, I stay. I expect you'll come and see me."

"What I'm trying to say is that I shall soon be a man with a job and a salary. A man who can think in terms of permanence."

"What sort of job?" Jennifer asked without interest.

Hugo told her. She choked some wine back into her glass and let out peal after peal of laughter.

"My poor Hugo. Oh, my poor love. A *nurse-maid*."

At one o'clock that morning, Hugo said to the Junior Dean, "Harold, what am I to do about Jennifer? She won't take me seriously."

"Then don't take her seriously. Enjoy your immoral afternoons, but otherwise don't bother about her, and for heaven's sake do some work before your Tripos."

Harold poured himself a large glass of brandy and then reluctantly poured some for Hugo too.

"It's no good, Harold. I'm committed to more than immoral afternoons."

"She isn't. Why can't you make do with what you've got? A lot of people would be delighted with it."

"Because it isn't good enough," said Hugo. "It's incomplete. It is, somehow, a sort of blasphemy."

Harold took a long look out of the window. On the other side of the court was the chapel, with its elaborate aspirations towards heaven, which had been ordained by a pious founder. Over to his left was a long, cool building of much later date, a reminder, in its every line, of mundane elegance and reason. Not for the first time, Harold pondered the contrast.

"When I chose the academic life," he said at last, "I forgot one thing. That the young could be such vile prigs. Blasphemy, Hugo, is outside my terms of reference. But if it were a word I used, I should say that what *is* blasphemous is the way you are neglecting to use your very sound brain except to worry about a cheap little harlot."

31

"I don't think that's very kind, Harold… You're usually so tolerant."

"Kindness and tolerance," said Harold, "are not at all the same thing. Now drink up your nice brandy and go to bed."

The next day Jennifer, who had just started her monthly period, did not sport Hugo's oak and was almost sombre in her behaviour.

"If you must think about the future," she said uninterestedly, "there's a lot of things we shall have to get straight. But just for a start you'd better meet my father. He's coming at the weekend."

Although it was a Saturday and very hot, Jennifer's father wore a business suit and a Homburg. He seemed very concerned about the economics of the University, wondering aloud why it did not pay its own way and displaying (rather than expressing) resentment of its Government subsidy.

"Why is it so big?" he said of Trinity Great Court. "They're short of lodgings, I'm told. Why don't they knock down that fountain and build over the whole square?"

Hugo shuddered. Jennifer appeared not to have heard. They crossed the river and approached the University Library.

"What does that mean?" said Jennifer's father, pointing at the Latin inscription over the entrance to the new court of Clare.

"*Sui memores*," said Hugo, "*alios fecere merendo*: by their worthy deeds they ensured that others will remember them."

"Why can't they say so in plain English? And what 'worthy deeds'?"

"It is a quotation," said Hugo, "familiar to all men of even moderate education; and in this instance it refers to members of this college who died in battle to make the world safe for big business."

Mr Stevens chuckled patronizingly. "I like a lad with spirit," he said. Jennifer took her father's arm and snuggled against his shoulder.

"You mustn't tease Hugo, Daddy. Cambridge and everything in it means a lot to him, doesn't it, Hugo?"

"Yes," said Hugo shortly.

"This library," said Mr Stevens, looking at it with hatred: "Is it one of those that gets sent a copy of everything that's ever printed?"

"Yes."

"Where do they put it all?"

"There is an extensive basement. And they send a lot of it for storage elsewhere."

"What do they want it all for?"

"Historical records."

" 'History'," said Mr Stevens, " 'is bunk.' Who said that? Come on, girlie, you're the educated one of the family."

Later that evening, while Jennifer was in the Ladies', Mr Stevens said to Hugo, "You going steady with my girl?"

"You could call it that."

"Well I hope you're not filling her head with a lot of rubbish. I didn't want her to come here at all, you know, for fear of the rubbish she might pick up."

"Why did you send her then?"

"She wanted to come. She gets her way with me."

"She is certainly strong-minded. I don't think she'll pick up very much…'rubbish'…of the kind you mean."

"You've got a head on you, I can see that," said Mr Stevens, "for all your Latin and gobbledy-gook. What are you going to do when you leave this place?"

"I'm going to be a schoolmaster."

"No money in it."

"I shall be a sort of partner in the school."

"That's better then. But if I thought Jennifer wanted you for keeps, and if you had the right stuff, I could do better than that for you."

"I shall be quite happy, thank you."

"Dedicated, eh?"

"No. Just involved."

'Well I suppose you know what you want. But I want what's good enough for Jennifer, and that doesn't fit in with the schoolmaster lark."

"She'll decide about that for herself."

"She will," said Mr Stevens; "but there's a lot of her father in her."

What am I doing with these people? I haven't the smallest thing in common with either of them, except the one pleasure which I share with Jennifer. Why, then, do I try to lend her significance beyond that pleasure? Why don't I just do as Harold says – take what she is prepared to give and ignore the rest, which is so palpably not worth the having? Perhaps I am trying to excuse myself for what I do with her – to convince myself that it really does involve more than just *that*. Or perhaps I am trying to excuse her. And yet I am no puritan; I should be capable of enjoying sex by and for itself. Why then do I feel so committed to her when I know that in her sexuality alone does she have any value?

Am I in love with her? But how could I love anything – yes, any *thing* – so mean and vulgar? Perhaps I am what they call infatuated. That is the word which they use in application to people like Jennifer. But whatever it is, I don't want it to stop, now or ever; for she fills not only my loins but my whole being with excitement, until I feel a kind of *spiritual lust* for her. She is, after all, near perfect in her kind. The very essence of vanity, the most apt embodiment of futility and physical greed. It may be that she has that same and unnameable quality which drove Catullus to grovel before Lesbia and Troilus to pawn his honour among the tents.

"I thought you once told me your father was rather rich," said Hugo.

"So he is."

"You implied that he was rich without working. I still don't know what he does, but it is clear from his demeanour…that he does something."

"He's in the city… Turn over, will you," Jennifer said, "I just want to see whether – "

" – What in the city?"

"Does it matter?"

"Not really. Whatever it is has given him some pretty poisonous attitudes."

"Just because he doesn't know Latin? And hasn't much time for a set of draughty old buildings?"

"Those are only symptoms. The disease goes deeper."

"So now my father's diseased, is he?"

Jennifer swung her legs off the bed and slapped her feet on to the floor.

"You prig," she said: "you horrible prig. Just because Daddy doesn't go all gooey every time someone says two words in Greek."

She pulled up a stocking and clipped it into place with two vicious snaps.

"And let me tell you this," she said, ripping her knickers on with the fury of a tricoteuse, "whatever your ideas for the future may be, mine don't include running round with a lot of little boys and wiping their noses every five minutes. Anyone I marry must either be rich or at least do a proper man's job – like Daddy. So goodbye for now, Miss Hugo Warren, and don't forget to see that all the little dears do a pee-wee before they go to bed."

But the next day after lunch she was back again. Their afternoon love-making, which no longer had the magic of exploration but was rendered ever more exciting by the gradual perfecting of spectacular skills, continued without interruption until the start of Hugo's exams and was renewed as soon as these were done. But nothing more was said of the future;

Jennifer behaved as though it did not exist, and Hugo thought it wiser to keep his own counsel for a time. And so the grass grew thick in the meadows over the river, the scholar's year waned as nature's waxed, and they came to the month of June.

IV

With june came Lionel, to play cricket for the Greenjackets in the annual match against the college. Hugo had cried off a lot of college matches so far this summer, as they conflicted with afternoon love-making; but he asked for and was given a place in the team for this one, despite the objections of Jennifer.

"A whole day's fucking gone west," she said.

"It was longer during the exams."

"That couldn't be helped."

"Nor can this. My cousin Lionel's coming."

"Oh fuck your foul cousin. And I suppose you'll have to spend the evenings with him. Talking about which boys are wetting their beds and who's got the newest pubic hairs."

"I doubt whether Lionel will want to discuss that. But I shall be spending the next two evenings with him. Both teams dine together, you know."

"I didn't know. I hope the food chokes you and your bloody cousin gets hit in the crutch by a cricket ball."

But her ill humour was somewhat allayed when he told her of the arrangements he had made for them to go to some of the May Balls the following week.

"Daddy's given me a dress to make them all spit with envy," she said. "It comes right down my dugs to the nipple."

When Jennifer had left him, Hugo went to the station to meet Lionel.

"Looking rather pale," Lionel said. "No cricket?"

37

"Not as much as usual. Working for the exams."

"How did they go?"

"Fair," said Hugo uneasily; "I was unlucky over the questions."

"Never mind," said Lionel, "there's nothing to be done about it now. You'll be playing in the match tomorrow?"

"Oh yes. And tonight Harold's giving a party for both the teams."

"Just like the old days," said Lionel, smiling long and gently with his eyes.

Since most of the cricketers were relatively moderate men, Harold and Hugo were the only two people who got drunk at Harold's party. Hugo, indeed, got crying drunk, and said nothing to anyone from eleven o'clock onward; but Harold just became more and more loquacious, until even Lionel was hard put to it to go on listening to him with patience.

"When I was a boy," Harold said, "we had a sense of proportion. Of discipline. We had our love affairs, yes, but we did not bore our friends by telling them how miserable we were, and we found time to get on with our work. But these days they just dissolve into a *mess*. Look at that cousin of yours, Lionel. Too drunk to talk, too fuddled with sex to read a page of Greek the entire term. And all over a cheap little girl who ought to be selling peanuts in a cinema. No self control, you see. And do you know why he's got no self control?"

"Why?" said Lionel obediently, while Hugo sat in a corner glaring straight ahead at nothing.

"Like all the rest of them, he takes himself too seriously. Which is to say he thinks in terms of what the world can or should offer him, instead of what he could or should offer to the world. It's the great obversion of the age. They all require to be spoon-fed, to sit there and have it brought to them on a tray instead of going out to find it for themselves."

"Find what for themselves?"

"Whatever they want. Whatever they want, they think *it* ought to come to *them*, and then they complain if it isn't precisely the quality and quantity they wanted."

One by one the cricketers said good night and drifted away over the court.

"In a way," said Lionel, "I agree. Hugo once excused himself to me on grounds of the importance of 'life'."

"That's it. Life. Sit there on your bum and let 'life' lap you round and do it all for you. Forget that you've got a brain, or a pair of hands, or a penis, to use as you alone see fit. Glittering prizes for glittering swords, *et cetera*, that's all out of the fashion now. *That* would be aggressive or something. So just sit there and wait for what comes and whine if you don't much like it."

Hugo leant out of a window and was noisily sick.

"See what I mean? No discipline."

"I think," said Lionel, "it is time we were going to bed."

"Bed. Rank sweat of an enseamed bed," said Hugo hoarsely.

"Come along, old chap."

"Nurse-maid," mumbled Hugo, "going round to see they don't wet their enseamed beds. God."

"Come along... That's it... Good boy."

"Good boy being put to bye-byes by nursey. Hold my hand, nursey. Make me do a pee-wee or I might wet the bed. Goo-night. Goo-night."

"No sense of proportion," said Harold, and flicked a blob of sick off the window-sill and into the court below.

"Do you often drink as much as you did last night?" said Lionel on the way to the cricket match.

"Not really," Hugo said shiftily. "Last night I was under pressure. The strain of those exams, and then...well..."

"You mean this girl Harold was talking about?"

Silence.

"Of course," said Lionel, "since I don't know much about it, I can't really help. But if you want my advice — "

" – I don't, Lionel. Don't advise me and don't preach at me. Just mind your own business."

"Very well," said Lionel, turning a dull red, not from anger but from sorrow.

"Just don't interfere," Hugo went on: "don't try to find out more and don't start conspiring with Harold. Just leave us alone."

Then they came to the cricket ground, which was surrounded by tall trees, rather like the ground at Baron's Lodge, and which flickered in the morning heat.

The Greenjackets batted first, and by three o'clock had declared with 292 runs on the board, sixty-five of which had been soundly and cannily contributed by Lionel. Hugo, who was still sulking, had fielded poorly and had sat down as far as possible from Lionel at lunch. When, during the interval between the innings, Lionel came over to talk to him, he muttered something about "padding up" and disappeared into the pavilion. When Lionel followed him, he went into the lavatory and locked the door.

I'm being childish, he told himself; but then Lionel's nothing but an overgrown schoolboy himself.

The college innings began badly, and by the time Hugo went in his side had scored only sixty-odd runs for the loss of four wickets. If Hugo himself failed, there was precious little batting to follow. Although Lionel, at short leg, was smiling and trying to catch his eye, Hugo set his face and ignored him. He took a look round the fieldsmen, turning his eyes in a slow arc from mid-off to third man, and then again from deep leg to mid-on, and deliberately withholding, as his gaze passed over Lionel, any trace of response to his now openly pleading smile.

The first ball he received was just short of a good length and pitched outside the off stump. Hugo played back to it and found, in confirmation of what he had observed from the pavilion, that the bowler was bringing the ball in from the off. There was no sting in the delivery, no difficulty about its flight, no altered pace off the wicket: just standard off breaks, Hugo thought, which, if hit with the spin, would disappear over mid-wicket's head as inevitably as ghosts recalled by cockcrow. And so, when the second ball he received was well up to him and slightly outside his leg stump, he moved his left foot into the line and swung his bat with great power in a shot which was somewhere between an on-drive and a leg-sweep.

The ball, struck from the meat of the bat, hit Lionel where his right hip neared his groin, just where, years before, a bullet had found him as he fought in Normandy.

For a moment he stood quite still, the smile of pleading clear on his face; but before Hugo could answer the smile, first Lionel's face, then his whole body sagged into a limp heap of white, discarded on to the green grass like the underwear of a drunkard on his bedroom floor.

V

"I've told you a hundred times," said Harold, "It wasn't your fault. Lionel died of a cerebral haemorrhage. This *could* have been brought on by the shock of the blow, but it could equally well have been coincidental."

"You know it wasn't coincidental."

"I don't, but even then you're not to blame. It was a pity the ball hit Lionel just where he had been wounded, but don't tell me you deliberately aimed it at his groin."

"If only we hadn't quarrelled like that. There was Lionel, following me around all day like a great big faithful dog, begging to be forgiven, when it was me that ought to have been begging. How could I have been so *infantile*? And then this…"

"It is not a bad thing," said Harold coolly, "to assume that all one's friends may die the next minute. It happens quite often as one gets older, and if one is always considerate of them, one is not a prey to guilt when it does. Remember the rule – and then forget your silly fracas with Lionel. It didn't go deep enough to count."

"Is that all the comfort you have to offer?"

"I've told you you were not to blame. Why should I have any more to spare for you just now?"

"You are my friend…and you were Lionel's."

"As your friend, I've done my best to relieve you of irrational guilt. As Lionel's, I have sorrow enough of my own without taking on the burden of yours."

"But don't you understand, Harold? When Lionel became unconscious, for the last time, he still thought I was angry with him. We parted in anger."

"Parted? What have you learnt in three years at this college? There was no 'parting', Hugo. Lionel has ceased to exist. Before he ceased to exist be was slightly uneasy because you and he had had a mild tiff – which was at least partly his own fault. Now it doesn't matter because there is no Lionel to carry away the memory."

"I am still here to retain it."

"You also retain other memories and better ones. Think of those if you will. But remember that no memories whatever can change your relationship with Lionel, for good or ill, because since there is now no Lionel there can no longer be a relationship. Whatever relationship there *was* stays unaltered by his death. If it gave you no guilt when he was alive, there need be none now."

"Suppose I was always guilty, but that it took his death to make me know it?"

"Then I cannot help you," said Harold, "and you cannot expect me to. Stop demanding, Hugo. When is the funeral?"

"The day after tomorrow at Baron's Lodge. You'll be coming?"

"Yes," said Harold. "A funeral has no relevance except as a sanitary office, but I think James and Georgy would like it…

Jennifer sported the oak.

"Come on," she said.

"I… You've surely heard what's happened?"

"Come on."

Hugo looked at her, then sat down heavily on the sofa.

"Very well," she said.

Competently and swiftly she unbuttoned his shirt, then her own blouse, then his trousers. She put her hands to the zip at

43

the side of her skirt, but suddenly changed her mind and hauled it up to show the naked thighs above her stockings.

"Here," she said, "like this. Randy parlour-maid and the son of the house. In a hurry because Mummy's expected home."

She straddled over him and lust leapt between them like a forest fire.

Although the graveyard on Church Straight was officially disused, the Escome family still owned a substantial plot in it which had been bought by James' grandfather; and it was here, among the nettles and the blackberry bushes, that they buried Lionel. As James had observed, halfway through the third large whisky with which he was fortifying himself for the ceremony, it was what Lionel would have wished.

The rector, an old rowing blue, was now recommending the life to come in the hectoring tones of a regimental sergeant-major. Believe this, he seemed to be saying or else Lionel, of course, could not hear him. Of those that did, there was not one who thought the life to come would be very pleasing to Lionel; there was no cricket, and the conversation of the seraphim, etc., was apparently confined to repeating the word Hosanna in tones far louder than good manners would have permitted elsewhere.

The boys had all been sent away for a day's picnic, in three coaches and under the care of the least cretinous of the young masters. The funeral was private; apart from the family only Bessie and Harold were present, though a few unsolicited tributes had been sent up from the town. As they stood by the grave, James, whose face was blurred with tears and alcohol, staggered badly and might even have fallen in, had not Georgy and Bessie, stationed on either side of him, each seized an arm. Hugo and Harold stood slightly behind the other three. Harold, though his eyes were dry and his face set, was crying inside himself in a series of spasms. Hugo, at first numb, then began to think of Jennifer with her skirt raised to show the smooth thighs above her stockings, and had to shift his position lest the rector should see the erection which must, he thought, be discernible through his trousers.

But the priest's attention was engaged in trying to make the undertaker's men realize that it was now time to lower the coffin. They were pretending not to know this in order to annoy him, one of the ways they used quite often to repay him for his inconsiderate and overbearing attitudes in daily intercourse. Another way was to let the coffin tilt as it was lowered, a trick which they threw in for good measure on this occasion. However, despite being all but deposited on his bonce, Lionel was eventually fitted snug and Bristol fashion into his long home, leaving the rector at liberty to embark on the series of platitudes, half minatory and half patronizing, with which he was wont to wind up affairs of this nature.

Clergymen, thought Hugo, are all politicians at heart; they cheerfully arrogate to themselves and their God the credit for anything nice which may occur, and then, in time of trial, busily demonstrate that all unpleasantness is due to the ineptitude of others.

No one had yet discussed with Hugo his part in Lionel's death. They were waiting, he knew, till after the funeral. Then they would ask him what had happened, tell him, as Harold had, that he was not to blame, and wait for him to accuse himself and beg their forgiveness. James, who would get much drunker, would bother him least of all; Georgy would blackmail him with sympathy and understanding; Bessie would call on him, as a matter of decency and common sense, to own up. Nor could Harold protect him, for Harold that day had his own battles to fight.

The rector reverted to prayer for the grand finale. "For as much as we, born from sin and into vanity, are still Thy children…" Hugo realized with relief that his erection had subsided; Bessie would certainly have noticed it on the walk back. "…And receive him into the life eternal. Amen."

Amen. Finis. So what possible good talking about it? It was not to be borne, what they were all getting ready for him with the best of intentions, and he had better leave. Harold would want to get to Cambridge – he was an examiner for the Tripos and had hundreds of uncorrected papers still on his hands – and Hugo would say that Harold must have company on his journey back. No one would be deceived but the decencies would have been upheld. So long as no one connected his departure with Jennifer, with whom he was to attend the Trinity May Ball the following night, they would not think too hardly of him. Some face-saving formula like "Needs time to sort it out" would be arrived at. They would see him go sorrowfully but not disdainfully, only Bessie perhaps implying that he had once more shown lack of character. As long as nobody knew that it was Jennifer who was taking him from them at this time... But no one knew of her at all except Harold, who would be too preoccupied, if not too charitable, to put two and two together, and who would in any case be too loyal to say anything. Yes, he would offer to accompany Harold back to Cambridge that very afternoon and would make a vague promise to return in two or three days.

But things did not turn out at all as Hugo would have wished. To start with, Harold showed every sign of meaning to stay till the following morning. This would still give Hugo ample time to meet Jennifer for the Ball but it would also give Georgy and Bessie a whole evening in which to get at him. And clearly they did not intend to waste time. Hardly had the rector been got rid of and the tea things cleared, when Bessie took James up to his room to rest and Georgy asked Hugo to come with her into the garden.

"What time do the boys get back?" he said fatuously.

"About six. Hugo – "

" – How have they taken it?" he persisted.

"It's difficult to tell with children that age. Some of them are very upset. Hugo, you *must* tell me. Exactly how did this terrible thing happen?"

"I hit a cricket ball extremely hard," said Hugo in the flat voice he had rehearsed for this eventuality, "and by ill luck it caught Lionel on his old wound. He fell down unconscious, and when he didn't come to we sent for an ambulance. After he had been some time at the hospital they diagnosed a cerebral haemorrhage. He died six hours later without regaining consciousness."

"Oh… Poor Lionel… Poor Hugo."

"Harold," said Hugo stiffly, "is of opinion that the blow and the haemorrhage were not necessarily connected. But somehow this seems unlikely."

"Even so, you can't blame yourself."

"Not logically, no. But I doubt if anyone can remain strictly logical in a case like this."

"You must trust us, Hugo."

"I can't even trust myself."

"If you want to make everyone even more unhappy, then to talk like that is the best way of doing so. We must all try to forget what has happened and go on as before."

God damn you to hell, Hugo thought. And then: if she will persist in forgiving me, there's only one way out. Crush her. That will be too much even for *her* understanding nature. She'll have to be crushed, perhaps they'll all have to be crushed, before I can be free.

"I knew you'd say that," he said carefully. "But I want to make people unhappy. Myself most of all. Do you know why?"

"No."

"Because so far I haven't been able to. Not really. I've worked myself into states, I've made scenes with Harold, I've invented attitudes, but I haven't been able to feel one particle of real regret. I kept begging Harold for comfort which I didn't need.

Because I didn't care. Even though Lionel and I had quarrelled bitterly before he died, I just didn't care."

"He wouldn't want you to be remorseful," said Georgy doubtfully.

"But *I* want to be remorseful. Otherwise I shall begin to doubt whether I exist."

She shook her head, but whether in negation or from incomprehension he could not tell.

"You must try to realize what I'm saying," he went on urgently. "It's not just Lionel. All this term I've been engaged in making myself cheaper and dirtier than I would have thought possible, but I can't feel the faintest remorse over that either. I've neglected my work, though really I like it. I've been abominable to Harold, I've done things more disgusting than you could imagine; but I can't feel, though I want to feel, that any of it matters in the slightest. Let me tell you, Georgy dear, what I've done…"

And without omitting the smallest detail he told her of his love-making with Jennifer: of its elementary beginning, its swift and complex development, of the assiduity and expertise with which it was still conducted. He spared her no gesture however gross, no refinement however perverse. Her face, at first blank, crumpled into little twitches, and by the time he had finished her eyes were pouring with tears.

"Why do you tell me this?" she said.

"Because I want you to know that I am both truly vicious and also incapable of feeling guilt. On a superficial level, I understand the proposition that such and such practices are disgusting, that such and such a way of life is unworthy. But I cannot *believe* this in any important way, just as I cannot find the practices in question anything other than wholly delightful. Nor have I any confidence in what, by contrast, I am supposed to credit with excellence. I can find no virtue in virtue, Georgy – and I only wish I could. All this may make it easier for you to understand any unexpected decisions I may come to later."

Harold came round the rose bushes.

"James would like to see you," he said to Hugo.

"Is he sober?"

"Approximately. He wants to talk to you because he misses Lionel and conceives that you have already taken his place."

"I can't talk to Uncle James now," Hugo said. "In a day or two, but not now."

"You must. He's waiting."

"Not today, Harold."

"Please, Hugo," Georgy said, her face averted to hide her tears from Harold.

"I'm telling you both. Not now and not today. I don't know about Harold, but I'm going back to Cambridge. There's a train to London in half an hour. Harold?"

"No, Hugo, no," moaned Georgy. "You can't... *Why?*"

"In Cambridge things may become clearer. Here there's just a fog of whisky and female hysteria."

"And you'll leave James like this?" said Harold. "Desert him?"

"Anything rather than be pitied for guilt I can't feel and be made to grovel for forgiveness I don't want."

"We don't want you to ask for forgiveness. We just want you with us," Georgy implored.

Hugo shrugged and started to walk away.

"Hugo has already found a new tune," remarked Harold dully. "A day or two ago in Cambridge he merely wanted me, or so he said, to exorcise a commonplace feeling of remorse. Now he pretends to a deeper guilt – accidia, moral indifference – , because only something as powerful as this can relieve him from such harrassing practical duties as comforting your father. It is an ingenious escape mechanism, I grant him that."

"He's only upset," said Georgy, "that's all. Come back, Hugo," she called, "come back."

But Hugo was already inside the house. He went upstairs, picked up his case, and ran down to the front door. As he opened it, three coaches full of boys came up the drive. One or two boys looked at him curiously, others, who knew him better, waved through the windows with, as he thought afterwards, an odd mixture of gaiety, encouragement and humility, rather as though they hoped he had come to protect them from something, to be their champion in some crisis which they knew to exist but did not properly understand. At the same time, Bessie came out of the door behind him.

"Off already, lad?" she said coolly.

"I'll be back. Two, three days," he mumbled.

The boys were already dismounting. Afraid of delay and wishing to be rid of Bessie Hugo set off quickly down the drive, carefully avoiding the boys' hurt and disappointed eyes.

"I'll keep your bed made up then," Bessie called after him.

He raised his free hand in salute but did not turn. In less than a minute he was walking down Church Straight towards the station, past the graveyard where the undertaker's men were still shovelling the earth on to Lionel's coffin.

Jennifer munched her way through a large plateful of cold salmon. She was getting up her strength, as she called it, for the Trinity Ball.

"Nothing but salmon in May Week," she said when she had finished, "I'm sick of the sight of it. Hugo dear… This cousin of yours that's dead…?"

"What about him?"

"He was the most important man at your school, wasn't he?"

"In effect, yes."

Jennifer looked as though she were going to pursue the subject but tackled a cold breast of chicken instead.

"All this cold food," she said, "bad for a girl's digestion."

Hugo looked out over King's Parade. Late as it was, workmen were still shuffling in and out of King's with bits and pieces of the marquee for the King's Ball, which would happen the evening after next.

"I've got the tickets for the King's Ball all right," said Hugo. "Still want to come?" he asked, never doubting the answer.

"We'll see."

"See? But you said…hardly a week ago…"

"We'll see, Hugo. A girl can have too much of a good thing."

"Look here, Jennifer – "

" – Don't start a quarrel, Hugo dear. We've got a nice evening in front of us, so let's make the best of it. You're always so worried about what's going to happen tomorrow or next week."

"Those tickets cost six guineas."

"Don't be mean. And order some more champagne. All this food's enough to choke one."

After more champagne and two large brandies Hugo's composure was restored. He had arranged for Jennifer and himself to join a party in the rooms of a Trinity friend, and thither they went down an avenue of fairy lights which Jennifer admired but Hugo secretly thought a desecration. When they arrived the party was just finishing its dinner; Hugo and Jennifer were welcomed with little screams and were settled on a window seat with a bucket of champagne between them.

"Very cosy… Jennifer…"

"Yes?"

"I shan't go back to Baron's Lodge. Not ever. If you don't want me to."

"Think of tonight, Hugo. Not next year."

"But aren't you pleased?"

Their host came up to them carrying two bottles of champagne under either arm.

"Harry champers?" he said. "You're being very slow. We all thought we'd have a dance or two and then take a look at those punts they've got on the river. And if anyone gets thirsty, there's a dozen bottles on ice over there and more in the bedroom." He belched emphatically. "So if you must use the bedroom, you're liable to be interrupted by fellow bacchants foraging."

He winked, leered, and staggered back into the arms of a tall girl with a voracious county face, who carted him off to dance.

"Punts," said Jennifer to Hugo. "Let's find a punt."

As they walked towards the river, Hugo said, "Were you pleased by what I told you? About not going back to Baron's Lodge?"

"What will you do instead, Hugo?"

"Get a job. Industry's crying out for university graduates."

"Who know nothing but Latin and Greek?"

"They think we make good administrators."

Since it was very early in the Ball they had no trouble in getting a punt. Hugo paddled up river; past wide lawns and weeping willow trees, under grave bridges, then through a reed-fringed pool which lay beneath a lock, and off into a tributary channel. Guiding the punt carefully, he edged it between the bank and a curtain of drooping branches.

"You'd never make it in industry," Jennifer said.

"Why not? I was quite efficient in the army."

"You enjoyed being an officer and a gent. Industry wants something different."

"There are other things. The BBC... Publishing..."

"You haven't the persistence for the first or the money for the second."

"You're not very encouraging," he said. "After all, I'm doing this for you."

"No, you're not. You're doing it because you daren't go back and face them at that school."

"I want to get away from Baron's Lodge because I want something bigger. And to prove to you that I'm capable of something bigger."

"There's only one thing now," Jennifer said, "that I want you to prove."

She jerked herself forward from her reclining position and nuzzled her cheeks against his thighs.

"Go on," she said, and nipped him lightly with her teeth, "prove it."

On the way back, under the wooden bridge which crosses the river at Queen's, Jennifer said.

"That's your lot, Hugo."

"I beg your pardon?"

"That's your lot. You've just had the last little treat you're getting."

"I don't understand."

"I'm leaving you, Hugo."

"I still don't understand." He felt nothing; with his mind he had taken in what she had said, but as yet it had not even touched his emotions. The champagne, or the calmness which follows sexual satisfaction, or perhaps the mere mechanical problem of paddling straight – any or all of these kept him from feeling anything at all. He simply considered, from a purely intellectual point of view, the incongruity of her announcement.

"Why?" he said.

"You've begun to smell of bad luck."

"But you can't leave me now," he said. "In the middle of the Ball. In the middle of the river."

"I don't mean this very minute. At the end of the Ball. At dawn."

"And what makes you think I want to be with you until then?"

"Suit yourself," she said. "If *you* don't..." She cocked her head like a whore motioning from a brothel window.

Even now his appreciation of the matter was still only an intellectual one. He was being cheated; he didn't seem to mind very much; but surely he owed it to himself to display some suitable reaction?

"You bitch," he said, "you foul little bitch."

He lifted the paddle from the water, poised it in his hand like a spear, and threw it towards her dim, reclining figure. There was a sharp crack, a cry of pain.

"You remember where the party was," he said. "No doubt you'll be able to get back by yourself."

Then he half dived and half lurched off the punt, swam some fifty yards down the river, and dragged himself on to the bank by the bridge in King's. Looking back towards the punt, he saw nothing for a while; then, slowly and smoothly, the punt emerged from the shadows. In the stern was Jennifer, sitting firm and straight, paddling with grace and skill. If she saw Hugo, she gave no sign, but continued, with increasing speed, on her way back to Trinity Ball.

The next morning Hugo learnt that he had been placed, as a result of his performance in the Tripos examination, in the Third Class.

Dear Hugo, (Georgiana wrote from Baron's Lodge)
We've been hoping to hear from you about when you'll be coming back. Daddy says not to rush you, but I feel I must write and tell you something of our situation.

Daddy has taken Lionel's death even harder than I feared, and quite frankly it's going to be a very difficult job getting through to the end of the term. It's as though we'd suddenly been deprived of *both* the senior masters at one blow. The junior men were never more than barely adequate, and without effective direction they won't even be that. Mercifully, the scholarship and common entrance exams are all over – and the results quite good; but as you know there are a lot of things that need doing over the next month to wind up the school year, and in particular there are one or two occasions like the Fathers' Match which are important from the point of view of what Lionel used to call 'public relations'. As things are, I can't feel that a good impression will be made. It's not just that

Daddy is drinking much too much. A whole part of his mind seems to have left him, so that when people talk to him, even old friends, he often just stares at them as though he were wondering who they were and why they bothered. The only person who can do anything with him is Bessie, and indeed if it weren't for her I don't know how we'd manage at all.

And another thing. You remember I was talking to you about a certain Mrs Hunt and the way I thought she was making trouble because Daddy wouldn't take her son? Well, now I'm certain of it. Several more of the tradesmen have given notice that they wish to run our accounts on a short term basis, and I'm sure she's at the bottom of it. Luckily this won't affect us till the autumn, but when the squeeze does start Daddy will need to make arrangements which at the moment would be quite beyond him. (Last Saturday he even missed a cricket match; the boys were very distressed and only partly reassured when Bessie told them he wasn't very well. And of course they've been quick to notice a lot else besides.)

Hugo, please come soon. With all this unhappiness our only hope is 'to close ranks' – another favourite expression of Lionel's, I wish they didn't keep coming to me – and help each other in every way. I'm sure there can't be anything – anything important, that is – to keep you at Cambridge. As for what you told me about that girl, I'm not jealous, but I don't think you should let her stop you coming back to us. Not now. And Hugo, if you like, if all that is so important to you, I promise you we can try again and perhaps this time it will be all right. Anyhow, please, *please* come home.

We read in *The Times* about your Third. Daddy said he'd hoped you'd do better but that it doesn't really matter to anyone. I hope you're not upset. I'm sorry this has been such a dreary letter. I'm sure things will take a turn for the better very soon. As soon, perhaps, as you come.

With all my love,

Georgy.

For a long time Hugo thought what it must have cost Georgy to plead with him so abjectly. Her confidences he was used to; but this went a long way beyond confidences; this was begging – and worse. Georgy was offering herself. He knew he should feel pity: he felt only disgust. He saw her again as she lay rigid and miserable among the sand dunes, then he poured himself a stiff drink and went to his desk and wrote:

Dear Georgy,

Thanks for your letter. I know things seem wretched at the moment, but that's because everyone's so miserable about Lionel. We must not confuse grief with need – a common temptation. So please don't think me unkind if I say that it's important that we should each of us face our own problems and stand up to them *for ourselves*; because it is at least possible that none of us will really have the energy left for coping with any problems other than his own.

Georgy, I have my own burden to carry. I told you the other day more about my character than I have ever told anyone. I also said that this might help you to understand any unexpected decisions I might come to. Well then. As things stand, it would be neither right, nor to anybody's true good, that I should return to Baron's Lodge. Never mind about finding a substitute for Jennifer, I could do without all that. It's just that it would be wrong, Georgy, for you and Uncle James and the school and myself, if, being in the state I am, I returned just now. My respect and affection for you all, not to mention common prudence, forbid it.

What was it that children – children at Baron's Lodge – held to excuse a deliberate lie? If you crossed your fingers while you spoke, he remembered, or if you afterwards pronounced "Hum hum", or some familiar infantile formula, even if only under your breath. "Hum hum" he said aloud to the empty room, and returned to his writing.

So I can't come back yet. Not till I've got myself sorted out. You must just accept this and forgive me if you can. I'm going away. Later on I'll let you know when I'm coming back. I'll try to see my way to this as soon as possible.

"Hum hum", he said again.

One practical detail of importance to all of us. I understand that there still remains a small amount of the money left for me in trust. According to Lionel, the trust was to be liquidated when my education was completed, and I presume that the remaining money is therefore available for use. *If* Uncle James wants to draw on this, to the extent of half the amount, he is very welcome. (This in case the tradesmen put on more pressure.) As for myself, I shall need some ready money in the next few months, so perhaps you could ask him to pay something fairly substantial into my account at the bank? I gather there should be about £2,000 left. So let us say that Uncle James is free to draw up to £1,000 if he needs it and that I would like £500 as soon as possible. Since he administers the trust there should be no difficulty about arranging this.

And so all my love,

Hugo.

And what could be fairer than that, he thought. Making them free of £1,000, just in case of trouble. Much more useful than his presence. And of course there wouldn't be any trouble. Why should there be? In a day or two they'd start to get over it all, Bessie would see to it that they made sense at the Fathers' Match, Uncle James would pull himself together and get an overdraft if he needed it, and everything could go on as before. They could easily hire someone to replace Lionel. It would cost a bit – but so had maintaining Lionel. Yes, everything could go on as before, he thought. But without me.

PART TWO

The Sport of Hermes

VI

Past a quacking guide, who begged to accompany him; past a
booth where he paid a surprising amount for a ticket; past an
unshaven official who inspected the ticket for a full thirty
seconds; past a notice which threatened dire prosecution should
he so much as put a pebble in his pocket; past a hundred and
seventy Americans with expensive cameras and whining
children, Hugo mounted to the Acropolis.

Good God, he thought as he gazed at the noon-day
Parthenon, is it possible to be so bored? For the first time in my
life I am visiting the source of civilization, of decency, truth and
letters, and I am finding it just a grinding bore. The walk, the
heat, the Americans, these piles of irrelevant stones – I wouldn't
mind so much if some of them were actively offensive. But
they're not; they're just an immense and irremediable bore.

It was now the middle of August. Late in June Hugo had
been notified by his bank manager that £500 had been paid
into his account by James Escome, though from James himself
or anyone else at Baron's Lodge he had heard nothing. Having
supplied himself with £450 in Bank of England notes, he had
flown to Paris and taken a train to Marseilles; from Marseilles
he had taken a boat to Genoa, from Genoa a train to Brindisi,
from Brindisi another boat to Corfu. At Corfu he had inspected
the villa of the Empress Elizabeth, got drunk, ineptly discharged
himself on a tired whore, and contracted gonorrhea. Having
been, as he supposed, cured by an Italian doctor, who advised

him to eschew alcohol for the next few weeks, he had proceeded by a succession of boats, each slower and dirtier than the last, to Leucas, to Cephalonia, to Ithaca, to Patras. In none of the first three places had he done anything but sit about or lie on his back, resenting his gonorrhea but still congratulating himself on his freedom. In Patras, however, boredom suddenly hit him like the floor of a slaughterhouse rising to a felled ox, so he got drunk on local brandy and treated himself to a whore even more tired than the one in Corfu. Two days later, in Corinth, he found himself with clap again, though whether it was a fresh dose contracted in Patras, or the Corfu dose washed back to the surface by bad spirits, he did not know. Nor, by that time, did he much care. He had, however, just enough prudence to see the necessity for a proper cure and just enough animation to hurry on to Athens to get it.

That morning, before his ascent of the Acropolis, he had been to an English-speaking doctor recommended by his hotel. Whatever might or might not have been diagnosed in Corfu or feared in Corinth, the doctor said, all he really had was an inflammation of the urethral tube which was due, not to a gonococcal infection, but to sexual strain. He was denied, it seemed, even the quasi-heroic distinction of having a proper dose. But how, he inquired, could one suffer from sexual strain when one's indulgence amounted only to two whores in six weeks? And why had the Italo-Corfiot practitioner misled him? As to the latter, said the courteous Athenian, he should remember that Corfu was empty half the year and that more could be charged for purporting to cure clap than for soothing a mere inflammation. And as for the inflammation or strain itself, this was just as likely to be caused by one act of clumsiness as by any amount of excess.

At least Jennifer had never caused him sexual strain. Even at her most predatory, Jennifer had never been clumsy. Although he did not miss Jennifer, he had in one sense almost forgotten her, he badly missed her skills; so that he often thought about her regretfully, not as an absent person, but as a forfeited series of high quality orgasms. So much, he now thought, for his "infatuation", let alone his "love"; the moral and spiritual nullity, which he had affected in order to escape from James Escome, was now beginning to prove real.

In any case Jennifer, whether as personality, stimulant or morality-gauge, was at the moment quite beside the question. The question was how a young man, sitting on the Acropolis in the heat of the day and having a tiresome case of urethral irritation, should counteract his loneliness and boredom. Sex, he had been told, was out for the time being; in drink (so far at least the Corfiot had been confirmed) he must be moderate. Well, so be it. There must be amusements other than alcohol and copulation; and when all was said, he had plenty of money. His fares had been reasonable, the cost of living in the islands had been derisory, the Italo-Corfiot, while no doubt deceitful, had not been greedy. He had £250 left, of which £50 at the outside would be enough for the journey home. The obvious thing to do was to buy a ticket to London and, having thus secured a line of retreat, devote the rest of the cash to pleasure. Certainly; but what sort of pleasure? And for how long? Did he want to eke out quiet amusements over many weeks, or blow the lot and return home? HOME? But where was Home, and what would he do when he got there?

He walked over to a platform on the ramparts, from which he could look out over Athens and towards the hills. All Greece is like these hills, he thought, a barren land and without comfort; by which lack of amenity scholars explain the courage and resource of the inhabitants; for the Greeks, having little help from nature, must help themselves. But he, Hugo Warren, had been reared in a different country, a lush country, where things were done for you and there was always milk on the doorstep. His home, if he had one, was in that country; to be precise, at Baron's Lodge. To return there would be to escape the harsh demands of these ungenerous hills; to return would mean an end of loneliness, a warm and grateful welcome, a steady and rewarding occupation, security for the body and peace for the spirit. But peace? Or was it atrophy? Whichever it was, he thought, it had more of dignity and purpose than accompanied most avocations. A schoolmaster, like an artist, could see the fruit of his labour; not just a figure on a bank statement but something which thought and breathed and which he, in a measure, had helped to mould. True, the comfortable rhythm of the academic year was apt to settle him in his ways, which explained why the distinction between peace and atrophy might at times be narrow; but they were honourable ways to be settled in and atrophy, at its worst, was a form of protection against many more positive evils.

What, then, was he trying to escape in this place? Better the green fields of Kent than these indifferent hills. It was futile to pretend, as he once had to Jennifer, that life (or these damned Greek hills) posed a challenge which he wished to meet. Even if there were such a challenge, even if there were in very truth something meaningful to be done, he was not the one to do it. So that his motive for not returning to Baron's Lodge could only be negative: it was not that he wanted something else or something bigger, it was just that he did not want Baron's Lodge. But then again, why not? He had just proved to himself what a satisfactory institution it was; and in the past, even in the very recent past, he had accepted and indeed almost relished the prospect of spending his life there.

But argue how he might, the idea of returning was repellent. He could give no concrete reason. The death of Lionel, the senility of James, the bossiness of Bessie, the pitiable fears and inhibitions of Georgy – none of these was the real reason, nor did they amount to a reason in aggregate. If he must try to explain, then the best he could do was to say, as Jennifer had said of himself, that Baron's Lodge had begun to smell of bad luck. Yes, that was it. The smell of age and whisky, of the damp earth waiting to be shovelled on to Lionel, of rotting boards in the neglected pavilion: the smell of bad luck. Indeed, this was the smell Jennifer had scented – not *his* smell but the smell of Baron's Lodge, a trace of which he had no doubt carried away with him after Lionel's funeral. By now the smell must surely have left him; nor would he return so that it might contaminate him once more.

So much, he thought, for rejection. Shun the bare hills of Greece and deny life's challenge: be wary, too, of the Kentish meadows and the comfort they seem to offer. But what is left to accept? Athena, goddess–guardian of this city, goddess–mother of wisdom, show me something which I may fittingly accept.

"Er…Warren?" said a polite but uncertain voice behind him.

He turned round to see a man, some five years older than himself, dressed in a light suit of fresh grey flannel. He was tall, nearly six foot and a half, with very fair hair and pleasant, regular features, behind which lurked some as yet unspecified form of weakness. With him was a woman, perhaps two years younger than himself, who would have been a taller and darker version of Jennifer, had she not sported a pronounced, an almost Roman, nose which lent her features and her whole immediate *persona* a massive respectability.

"Yes," said Hugo, "my name is Warren."

"I'm Nigel Palairet," said the man, "and this is my wife, Nancy. You may not remember, but we were at school together. Baron's Lodge. Early in the war. I was much older, of course…"

His speech, which had started firmly, had gradually trailed off into uncertainty. As this happened, the weakness that lay behind his eyes grew more and more apparent until it was almost as if he were pleading.

"Yes," said Hugo, "I remember you well."

Palairet, he thought. The Honourable NHS. A bit younger than Lionel. Eton, notable schoolboy racquets player, Carbinier Guards for his national service but just too late for the war, Christ Church, blues for Racquets and Royal Tennis. All this according to the Old Boys' page in successive editions of the Baron's Lodge Chronicle. No recent entries, however. Question: what happened after Oxford?

"And I may say," Hugo went on with genuine warmth, "it's very nice to see an approximately familiar face. I've just been feeling very fed up."

"All on your own?" asked Palairet.

"Yes."

"Us too. Of course it's not so bad with two of you, but a change is always nice. I mean – "

" – You mean you're bored with not having a man to talk to," said the girl. As she spoke her face broke into a smile which, Hugo thought, transformed its apparent severity into pure sweetness, but a sweetness which was disciplined, so that it could never become merely saccharine, by the strength of her nose and cheekbones.

"Hang it, Nancy," said Palairet, "it's nice to meet someone you were at school with when you're all this way from home."

"I was only teasing, Nigel. Now do the sensible thing and ask your chum to lunch. Then you can discuss the old days for as long as you like. I promise I shan't be bored."

"You'll have luncheon with us?" Palairet said.

"With the greatest possible pleasure."

As usual in Greece, the plates were cold and the food greasy; but it was nice to have someone (other than a tired Greek whore) to talk to. Since the past at Baron's Lodge was the most evident thing Palairet and Hugo had in common, they discussed it at some length. Then they moved on to Palairet's time in the Guards and at Oxford. The answer to what he had done since leaving Oxford was simple: he had done nothing. As a younger son, he had received a small lump sum (about £10,000, Hugo gathered) several years before, and the income from this, combined with a generous allowance which he was still paid by his family, had enabled him to wander about in some style while he was considering what to do next. This was a problem as he had no particular preference and no immediate motive; his degree was not good enough nor his title high enough to procure him glamorous employment, and there was no prospect of starvation to hurry him into any other sort. Then, a year ago, he had met Nancy, warmed to her (it hardly seemed more from what he said, nor did Nancy's presence inspire him to enthuse about the matter) and married her. Since then they had been on a sort of prolonged and desultory honeymoon. However, Nancy had brought no money to her wedding, he was beginning to make inroads into his capital (which was all the capital he would ever have) and clearly a new way of life must soon begin.

"Have you any ideas?" Hugo said.

"There is something. But it's all rather dubious. You see – "

" – I don't think," Nancy interrupted, "that we ought to discuss it. Not yet."

"I don't know," Palairet said; "among friends…"

Nevertheless, he spoke no more about whatever it was. Instead he questioned Hugo about his own plans.

"My position is very similar to yours," Hugo said, "except that I have much less capital to fall back on. I shall have to start doing something as soon as I get home."

"Didn't you say your cousin Lionel was dead?"

"Yes."

"Well, I don't know…I heard…I thought someone who knew you at Cambridge told me…you were going back to teach at Baron's Lodge. And with Lionel Escome dead, I should have thought…"

The weakness in his face was almost pitiful. But at the same time there was clearly a strange integrity in him which led him, as a matter of duty, to probe a disagreeable subject. This was the more surprising as in the present case the weak side of him could have pleaded "good manners" as a watertight excuse for avoiding the topic.

"Yes…" he persisted; "surely your uncle will need help. Now more than ever."

"It's not a thing I can take on," said Hugo. "I was going to, but I found I wasn't suitable. The school's in a very good way of business, and they can easily replace Lionel. I've discussed it all with my uncle. He says they can manage very well."

"Oh?" said Palairet.

"After all," Nancy put in, "it's not everyone that's suited to running round with little boys all his life."

"True enough," said her husband, "though it always seemed quite a decent occupation to me."

Still, he appeared to be more or less reassured by what Hugo had told him and referred to the matter no more.

"But what are you going to do *now?*" he asked Hugo. "Tomorrow. Next week."

"I was wondering about that when I met you. When I get home I shall have to find a job, but meanwhile I've got enough money to hang about for some time. It's just a question of whether I want to. And where."

Palairet glanced over at Nancy, who nodded mildly.

"Well," he said, "Nancy and I, we're going to drift slowly home. You know, Corfu, Venice, Milan…"

Hugo shuddered.

"What's the matter?"

"It's just that I once had a…regrettable experience on Corfu."

"Sorry about that. Perhaps we'd better miss it out. What I mean is, if you like, being all alone, why don't you drift home with us? The truth is, we haven't seen much of anyone for the last month or so and we'd both appreciate your company."

Hugo looked at Nancy, who confirmed what her husband had said with her enchanting smile. Steady, he thought to himself. There must be some catch here. Why, after two hours' conversation on the strength of a childhood acquaintance, should they suddenly ask me to join up with them? Are they really so lonely? Or are they broke? But whatever lay behind it all, it was some sort of an answer. A course of action, however vague, had been suggested.

"Yes," he said, "I'd like that. When did you think of leaving Athens?"

Two days later, their last before they left Athens, they went on an expedition to Delphi. On arrival, they were taken by their driver to what was reputedly the Pierian Spring and urged to drink.

"I suppose," said Nigel Palairet, "that one should drink deep or not at all."

Nancy and Hugo, sceptical, drank not. But Nigel went right down on his stomach and immersed his face in the brook, an awkward feat which he performed with surprising grace.

"Nigel can be very determined," said Nancy.

"Over trivialities like this?"

"He wouldn't regard it as a triviality. It is a tradition and must therefore be taken seriously."

Nigel rejoined them.

"You mustn't lose the opportunity," he said to Nancy. "Neither of you," he persisted, "it is unwise to offend the Muses."

Not for the first time, Hugo was reminded that once Nigel had got over his shyness, his speech, though apt to be sparse, had become pointed and articulate. Only when the three of them encountered strangers did he relapse into the diffuse and apologetic utterance which had characterized their first meeting.

"Come on," he was saying now, "you must drink."

"My stockings – "

" – Can be replaced. Come on."

"But really, Nigel – "

" – Drink."

He half raised his hand, so that for a moment Hugo thought he was going to strike her. And then suddenly Nancy was down on her knees, and Hugo beside her, both drinking the waters in deference to Nigel's sense of tradition. Afterwards, Hugo could never decide whether he had yielded to genuine authority or to his own desire to avoid a scene; and it seemed to him, though he did not care to question her, that Nancy was similarly in doubt.

On the way back from Delphi to Athens Nigel said, "It must have been hereabouts that Oedipus killed his father."

"You seem to know a lot about the place, Nigel."

"So should you. You read the Classics."

"Details of time and place were never my strong point."

"I'm making them mine," said Nigel. "For the future, they've got to be."

Since he showed no sign of explaining this almost Delphic remark, Hugo turned in question to Nancy. She shook her head, denying him. Riled, Hugo questioned Nigel directly.

"What can you mean?" he said sourly. "Are you opening a travel agency?"

"No, hardly that. I can't tell you yet," said Nigel kindly, "but I will when I feel I can."

But nothing further was said on the topic for many days.

When Nigel had spoken of "drifting" home it had been an understatement. They were going home a very long way round indeed, and for some time their drifting took them farther and farther east. Crete, Alexandria, Beirut; a day among the temples at Baalbek; an afternoon at the races; an evening at the Casino; a day doing nothing at all. But eventually they left Beirut for Cyprus, Cyprus for Corinth, and Corinth for Brindisi and Venice.

"Not stopping at Corfu, you'll be glad to know," said Nigel.

"You remembered?"

"I told you, dear boy. Details are my business."

"You've yet to tell me why."

"I will – when Nancy gives the word. She has an instinct for appropriate occasions. I am to be the expert on times and places; Nancy is to determine whether or not they are appropriate."

"With the assistance of the Muses?"

"I wouldn't go so far as to say that," said Nigel equably, "but it would have been impolite – don't you think? – to refuse what they offered."

In Venice they sat down outside Florian's. The murmur of the pigeons in the Piazza reminded Hugo of September in Cambridge, the season at which the pigeons moult in the empty Courts and there are no voices to drown theirs.

"We shall stay here some time," Nancy said. "Autumn has come, and there is an atmosphere of people returning home. It is a melancholy and rather pleasing atmosphere, but it can only be enjoyed by those who are staying still."

"Half way home now," Hugo said. "I'm glad I've been with you these last weeks…" He speared an olive with a little stake of wood. "I've been meaning to ask you, now I know you better. Why did you suggest that I came with you?"

"Largely for my sake," said Nigel.

"You see," said Nancy, "Nigel, like all Englishmen, enjoys the company of men. It is sometimes said that Englishmen dislike women, but this is simply not true. They like women well enough – but their upbringing places so much emphasis on male institutions and loyalties that the need for both lasts a lifetime. A sympathetic wife will see this need fulfilled."

"You are very generous," Hugo said, "most women are jealous even of their husbands' clubs."

"They are the greedy ones," said Nancy. "They want that part of a man which is not rightly theirs."

"They would say they had a right to every part."

"Which is why I call them greedy."

"And so I," said Hugo, "am the itinerant male element in Nigel's life? I am to make up for him for the absence here of White's or the Guards' Club?"

"And very pleasantly you do it," murmured Nigel.

"Thank you. In return for your kindness I must be frank. I am running short of money," Hugo said. "I quite agree that it would be nice to stay in Venice, but I for one cannot stay long."

Nigel looked at Nancy, who nodded assent as she had on the day of their first meeting in Athens.

"There is no need to worry about that," Nigel said.

"It's true I have a little money left in England from which I could pay back anything you lent me. But I'm not sure I can afford to spend it in this way."

"That is not what I meant," said Nigel. "You have waited very patiently for us to declare our mystery, and it is now time to do so. You may find that it has a leaning on your problem..."

At about the same time, Bessie said to Georgy at Baron's Lodge, "We'll be needing some more blankets, love. I've had to throw twenty of them out."

"Couldn't it wait, Bessie?"

"It can wait a week, love. Till the term starts."

"I'll talk to Daddy when he gets back from Canterbury."

"If he gets back sober."

"But he's only gone to watch cricket, Bessie. He'll be back by seven."

"They sell drink on cricket grounds, love, as you very well know. They have great tents full of it."

"I suppose I should have gone with him. But we had so much to see to here... Oh, Bessie..."

"There now, don't take on. He has good friends will meet him and see after him. Though what they'll think is another matter... You lie down for an hour or two, love, and I'll be busy with the sheets."

When James Escome arrived back from Canterbury he was rather glazed in expression but capable, as Georgiana supposed, of rational discussion.

"I shall have to buy a lot of new things this next week," she told him.

"What sort of things?" said James sullenly.

"We need some blankets for a start. Also some equipment for the kitchen. And this is surely the time of year, Daddy, when you ought to be buying some new footballs?"

"Lionel always took care of that."

"He won't now."

James walked to the sideboard and poured himself some whisky.

"If we get these things," he said, "there'll be bills at the end of the month. That's how it's to be now. And at the end of the month there won't be any money. Not when we've paid last summer's accounts."

"But surely, the bank...?"

"There's a new man there now. He says there's a thing called a credit squeeze. Government policy. He says he's been told not to give credit even against security."

"But he must. After all these years the account's been there."

"I reminded him of that. He apologized – none too nicely, I thought – and said we still couldn't have an overdraft."

"Then we must use Hugo's money. He said we could. It's only right he should help."

"You know we can't take Hugo's money."

James emptied his glass and returned to the sideboard.

"Very well," said Georgy, "I shall go to see the bank manager myself."

"If you like. But don't go talking to him about Hugo's money. I tell you it's not to be touched."

Georgy walked over to the french window, grasped the handle with her left hand and her left hand in turn with her right, digging her short fingernails hard into the flesh.

"Daddy," she said, "what arrangements have you made about...about masters for next term?"

"The young men are all coming back. And to do Lionel's work I've got a fellow called Gleason. Thirty years old, fair degree in the Classics, said to know something about games."

"That sounds all right" She had had to nerve herself to ask her question; now, relieved at the answer, she turned away from the window and faced James, who was sitting, slightly hunched, in an armchair.

"How can it be all right?" he said with sudden viciousness. "How can anyone take Lionel's place?"

"Of course no one can," she said soothingly. "But this Mr Gleason sounds as if he might be a help to us."

"He's a smarmy, ingratiating swine," James said. "If you ask me there's something fishy about him. But I couldn't inquire too closely because, you see, he's all we could get. The only man who'd come for the money."

"But for heaven's sake, Daddy. Whatever economies we make, whatever bills we do or do not pay, we *must* find money for proper staff. And even if the bank and the tradesmen are making things awkward just now, we've still got all the fees coming in three times a year. The school's full. It's only a question of adjusting our arrangements so that we pay small bills once a month instead of large bills once in four."

James took a long drink.

"You may as well know now as later," he said. "Fifteen boys have been withdrawn. Which means the fees we're getting for next term are about fifteen hundred pounds less than I'd expected."

"But...parents have to give notice before taking their boys away."

"They did. Before the end of the Summer term. They all had polite excuses. But what they meant was that Lionel's dead and Hugo's gone and I'm too old to carry on. They'd smelt out failure, Georgy. Particularly the women. Women have quick noses for failure. And for whisky," he added under his breath.

"But why couldn't you have told me? Bessie and I, we've been making arrangements as though – "

" – I couldn't face it. Anyway, I couldn't really believe it had happened. Some of the fathers were...I thought they were...old friends."

He rocked backwards and forwards, and then gradually buried his face in his hands.

"Never mind," she said, stroking his head, "never mind, Daddy. It'll come right, you see." And then, "Oh, Hugo, Hugo," she said in her heart, "why won't you come home?"

The new bank manager had a sharp ratty face and a manner which could be variously hectoring, insolent or servile, as occasion might require. Georgy, of course, did not qualify for a display of servility, but something about her demanded and received at least partial respect.

"I'd best be frank with you, Miss Escome," said the little rodent mouth. "The reason I gave your father for not granting him overdraft facilities was that the Government has asked us to be sparing with them; but at the same time, of course, it is at our discretion to make exceptions to the general rule, and in the case of old customers we are normally disposed to do so."

"Well then?"

"You must understand that banking is a business, Miss Escome. I am advised that your father is an old man, not – shall we say? – in the best of health, and that he has recently been deprived of assistance he counted on. These are bad auspices for a loan."

"It would only be a small one."

"The auspices remain the same."

"My father has engaged a highly qualified man in my brother's place," said Georgy, trying to state a fact and not to plead.

"Traditionally, Miss Escome, Baron's Lodge is a family concern. Or so they tell me. The engagement of an outsider in an important post is only one more sign of what I am compelled to call weakness."

"Very well," said Georgiana, "your help would have been appreciated but we can manage without it."

"I trust so," said the rat-lips. "Good morning, Miss Escome."

He did not rise to show her out, but nodded through a glass pane to an underling, who opened the door for Georgy from outside.

"Daddy," said Georgiana, "you mustn't be angry at what I'm going to suggest."

"Well?"

"If we took Mrs Hunt's son and some of her friends' – "

" – No," said James.

"But Daddy. It would mean we could fill some of the empty places. It would mean more money. And we'd have her on our side."

"I'm not going to grovel to that woman for favours."

"It would be us that conferred the favours."

"I'm glad someone can still think so. But it's too late in the day for her to set store by any offer we can make. And the answer is still no. No," said James, banging his fist down on the sideboard, "no, *no*, NO."

There was a knock on the door and Bessie came in.

"Listen to me, Mr Escome," she said. "You should not forget old friends when you're in trouble. You've been trying to keep things from Georgy and me, but now we know what there is to know. I've been laying money by for many years, and what should I be spending it on now? It's there and it's yours for the using, as long as you need it."

"No, Bessie," James began, "I can't, I – "

" – You can take it and be glad of it. And then, when things get right, you can give it me back. Meanwhile, we'd best be looking for young Hugo. It's time he was back here."

"We don't know where he is," Georgy said.

"He'll soon be back in England, wherever he is. That money he had won't last for ever. And when he's back, we must find him."

"No," said James. "He must come in his own time or not at all. I will not have him bullied or blackmailed. And that's final."

"Very well," said Bessie stiffly, "you're the master here. But surely," she added without a trace of irony, "you'll take the money? There's nigh on two thousand pounds. It'll make up what you've lost on the withdrawals."

James said nothing, but looked at Bessie and nodded. He did this without a sign of gratitude or hope; like a prisoner with a life sentence who takes his food from a warder, without pleasure or thanks but simply because he has long since formed the habit of accepting sustenance from somewhere. In this fashion James accepted Bessie's money, and for a time at least proper provision had been made for Baron's Lodge.

VII

When the three of them reached London late in October, Nigel said, "And now to business. Find out how much money you can raise, Hugo, and see that it's on hand. We don't need it yet, but you never know."

So Hugo wrote to his uncle and asked that the balance of his £2,000 capital should be paid into his own account. He had already had £500, he wrote, and he had authorized his uncle to draw up to £1,000; whatever James had already drawn he was welcome to keep, but Hugo would be obliged if he would draw no more as he himself now had a use for the money.

The next day Nigel handed Hugo a list.

"This is a list," he said, "of one hundred and fifty people. All of them are known to me personally or have been vouched for by others whom I trust. These people will form the nucleus of our…clientele."

"Let's have a look."

As Hugo had expected, the men and women on Nigel's list were drawn mostly from Nigel's own world. As he had also expected, quite a few of them were known to Hugo himself. What he had not expected was to find two or three of the most celebrated names in the kingdom.

"What will *he* say when he gets this?" said Hugo, pointing to an entry under "S".

"He's expecting it. He's one of the few people who knows exactly what's happening. Most of them have been sounded as to their theoretical reactions, but very few of them know we are actually on the point of beginning. In *his* case we had to make absolutely certain beforehand that he wouldn't be offended or kick up a fuss."

"Why didn't you just leave him out?"

"Very rich. A free spender. And if there should be trouble it might be useful to have a client with his connections."

"How did you get in touch with him?"

"Through a mutual friend." Nigel pointed to an entry under "B".

"Very nice reading." Hugo tapped the list. "How will you let them all know we're finally in business? And where to get hold of us?"

"Each person on this list will be visited in the next few days, the women by Nancy, the men by one of us. We shall tactfully explain the nature of our services and leave this card."

He handed Hugo an expensively printed visiting card. It bore the chaste legend, "Nigel Palairet. From November 11. 36, Chester Row. Sloane 2340."

"Supposing someone resents our proposals?"

"I've told you," Nigel said. "I know, or know of, all of them."

"You seem very sure."

"Of course. I've had a long time to work it all out. You see, Hugo, I'm not just in this for money. It struck me very early in life how wasteful it was that the world should offer such diverse pleasures but that so many people who would have appreciated them, who might have brightened their short grey lives with them, should be debarred from them by the pressure of official morality. I saw a vocation as well as a rich livelihood here. I must bring lovers of pleasure to their right true ends. So I spent years of travel and inquiry investigating two classes of people: possible clients, and possible agents of their entertainment. We weren't in the Near East just for culture when we met you."

This speech was an odd mixture of sincerity and irony. It was impossible to say where either began or ended. But Hugo was more concerned with the practical issues suggested by Nigel's reference to the Near East than with his philosophy of pleasure.

"You're surely not going to...to import?" Hugo asked.

"Only in a few very special cases. But one of our functions will be to provide clients who are fond of travel with a new supplement to the Atlas. A new kind of *Guide Bleu*, if you will excuse the pun. Hence my researches."

"Such information is soon out of date."

"I've arranged for it to be constantly checked and renewed."

"What does Nancy feel about all this?"

"She sees it as an interesting and rewarding occupation. She has no morals, only aesthetic preferences and personal loyalties, and she understands the need for money. Had she been any other kind of woman, I would not have married her. I find you sympathetic – and suitable for this work – for much the same reasons."

"I appreciate the thought."

"And of course," said Nigel gently, "it's nice to work with people one was at school with. It strengthens loyalty, and loyalty will be important to us all. Which reminds me. Have you heard how things are going at Baron's Lodge?"

"I rang up when we got home," Hugo lied. "My uncle said everything was in good order. They are all well and Lionel's successor has apparently made a good start."

"I'm glad to hear that," said Nigel, looking him kindly but closely in the eyes. "I was fond of James Escome and I was very happy at Baron's Lodge. I wouldn't like to think of things going wrong."

So Nigel was still concerned, thought Hugo, about the affairs of Baron's Lodge; and he would plainly hold Hugo in some measure responsible if these went wrong. Was there no escape? Here was a long established school with property and reputation worth tens of thousands of pounds; and just because something unexpected but entirely commonplace had occurred everyone seemed to think that the whole place might collapse overnight unless he, Hugo, hastened to its support. To be fair, Nigel himself couldn't think that or he would never have asked Hugo to join him; but even Nigel kept requesting Hugo's assurances that his uncle James was still all right.

How far, Hugo wondered now, would the facts bear out these assurances? Beyond writing to his uncle about money he had made no effort to communicate with Baron's Lodge, and as yet James had sent him no answer. But surely there was no cause for alarm? James had been given the use of £1,000, should he need it, from the end of June onwards; even now, he was not being required to repay anything he might have spent, merely to refrain from spending more. He could easily engage a master in Lionel's place, and had no doubt done so; the domestic staff, based round Bessie and Georgy, would presumably function as efficiently as ever; *if* more money were needed, it could surely be borrowed; and lastly, James' grief for Lionel must now be growing less painful. From a practical point of view Hugo would not – could not – be missed.

One then came to the moral side of the question. Well, he had told Georgy he was without moral sense, and the statement was becoming daily more true, so there was an end of that. And even if he were forced to a moral reckoning, he could point to what both Lionel and James had told him at different times – that he must not allow himself to be *blackmailed* into returning to Baron's Lodge. Since Lionel's death and Georgy's pleading might be said to constitute far stronger elements of blackmail than any previous, he was so much the more justified in his determination to resist.

Even so, he was not satisfied. Nigel, he remembered, had compared him to Nancy, who had – what was it? – "no morals, only aesthetic preferences and personal loyalties." And here he was caught both ways. If Baron's Lodge was indeed in danger, it was not to be tolerated, aesthetically, that such a calm and well rounded way of life should be disrupted. As for his personal loyalties, there could be no question where these were engaged. Never mind whether or not James and Georgy *should* be able to manage without him: the point was that they wanted him with them because they loved him and hoped that he loved them.

But again, what was all this if not another form of blackmail? It was not to be borne that such considerations should direct the entire course of his future. There was only one thing to be done. To protect his legitimate interests he must root out Baron's Lodge from his life: not just evade it, as he had been doing, but make it cease to exist for himself except as a mere name. After all, the mental adjustment should not be difficult; he had made a similar one when his parents died ("What were these two people to me?") and on other occasions since. If James and Georgy knew what was good for them, they would do the same thing to him as he was doing to them. Cut him out of their lives. And if they could not or would not do so, if they were going to cling or pester, then he would have to ask himself whether new and perhaps more ruthless methods might not be called for.

"What I don't really understand," said Hugo to Nigel a few days later, "is why you want to run gambling parties as well. I should have thought we had enough on our hands."

"The extra turnover will be helpful. And those present may take the opportunity to give us fresh…commissions."

"How shall you arrange the gambling?"

"Chemin-de-Fer and choice refreshments to give heart to the players."

"Croupiers?"

"Myself. I doubt whether we shall need to run more than one table. High gambling is a specialized interest."

"Where does our profit come in?"

"Very simple," said Nigel. "To play a single 'coup' at Chemin-de-Fer takes between two and three minutes. Every time a player holding the bank wins the 'coup', which on average is once in twice, i.e. once every five minutes, the house takes five per cent of his winnings. Standard practice. At the end of the evening, losers pay into the house, the house pays out to winners. But the amount we pay out will be less than what we take in to the extent of all the five per cents we've collected. Over a long evening's play this means a substantial profit."

"You give a definite undertaking to pay out all winners?"

"Yes. And correspondingly it will be most strictly understood that all losers must pay in to me. Not tomorrow or next week: at the end of the game."

"And if someone has chanced his arm and can't pay you?"

"This is one of the matters in which Nancy's intuition helps. She has a way of sniffing out welchers. But I don't expect much trouble over that – after all, our list is pretty exclusive… Which reminds me. Have you left cards on the people assigned to you?"

"All except ten. One of the chaps had dropped dead the day before, the other nine were abroad."

"Who's dead?"

"Colonel Willasey-Warburton."

"Poor Archie. He's never been the same since they pulled down Chelsea Barracks. Any trouble with anyone?"

"No. Enthusiasm, concealed excitement, indifference real or affected. No trouble."

"I told you… Tomorrow is November the eleventh. Armistice Day. Opening day. From tomorrow we no longer propose, we dispose."

"Why Armistice Day?"

"A day of good hope, don't you feel? And talking of hope, what about your money? I'd like to know how much we can rely on."

"I haven't heard yet," said Hugo awkwardly.

"There's been time enough."

"I'm sorry. I'll check up."

"Yes," said Nigel equably; "I should do that if I were you."

At Baron's Lodge autumn passed into winter. Although Bessie's loan to James had removed any immediate cause of anxiety, the empty desks told their own story. Nor had there been time, money or no, to find a more desirable new master than Gleason, whose presence and personality only emphasized the difference between the school as it was now and as it had been six months before. The boys, with the quick instinct of their kind, scented inadequacy or doubt; they became restless and even afraid, were resentful in their dealings with the staff, churlish and cynical among themselves.

Gleason's ability on the football field turned out to be purely nominal, and James himself had to take charge of the senior game. At first he had found this an interest and a distraction, for there were some promising players among the older boys; but as the weather grew damper and colder he needed more and more whisky to sustain his enthusiasm. Some afternoons even whisky could not help; James would remain moping in his study, while a junior master would be hurriedly dispatched ("Mr Escome is busy") to take the game in his place. If a minimal discipline was preserved, continuity was lost, and James' growing indifference was reflected in the boys' bored and listless play. The first eleven, from being one of the most promising in years, became a cowardly gang of malcontents and lost all but one of its first five matches.

One afternoon Gleason, who seemed to spend much of his time loitering in corridors smoking cigarettes, accosted Georgiana, who was on her way to confer with Bessie.

"I reckon your old man must have had half a bottle before lunch," Gleason said. "Young Waters is taking his game again. With a bit of luck he should just about keep control."

"It's a pity," said Georgy, "that you don't have quite your advertised qualifications as a footballer. You might have been able to help."

"Go on with you, missie. We all say we can play these games to help us into jobs. Don't tell me your papa was taken in. He had to have someone, and I was available at the price, and all talk of qualification was just gup."

"Tell me, Mr Gleason. Why did you leave your last job?"

Gleason scowled.

"It didn't suit me," he said. "There was a boy they said should have got a scholarship. But he didn't, and so they blamed me. It was his own fault, lazy little bastard, but they blamed me. I wasn't having that."

"And how are you finding the scholarship candidates here?"

"If they do what I tell them, they'll be all right."

"And do you find it difficult," said Georgy, "to make them do what you tell them?"

"Not me. I'm good at keeping order. Getting my own way. I'll show you."

He moved right up to her and placed his hands on her buttocks. Slowly, the cigarette still hanging from his face, he began to rub his body against hers.

"You like that, don't you?" he said. "Been waiting for it a long time, haven't you?"

"Let me go, please – "

" – Come on, tell us how much you like it, how you want it, all warm and – "

Georgiana pushed him away with a sudden thrust and walked on down the passage, desperately trying not to hurry.

"Needn't give yourself airs," the flat, common voice came after her, "your old man drinks, and you – you want it like hell, only you're too proud to admit it. You know where to find me, any time…"

His voice trailed off as she turned a corner and went on towards Bessie's door.

"Bessie, I – "

"What, love? Why, you're trembling all over, you're shivering. What is it?"

"I – It's nothing. I went outside without a coat."

If she told Bessie, Bessie would make her father dismiss Gleason. Loathsome Gleason might be, but at least he was a mature man and might help James keep some sort of order. If he went now, there would be no one else to come at this time of the year and the extra work and worry would kill James. Gleason must stay until the end of the term or until Bessie's money could be used to get someone better, and until then she must endure his insults.

"It's nothing," she repeated. "Just the cold."

Although Hugo had given James his address in London, the first letter he received from Baron's Lodge had been forwarded *via* Cambridge. It was from Bessie, who had plainly written it without telling either James or Georgy of her intention.

Dear Hugo, (she wrote)
I don't need to waste words. You're needed here and you must come. Your uncle can't do all the work and the man he's engaged is rotten. Things are bad, but they've yet to get so bad that you couldn't help to put them straight. There's no real difficulty about money; it's just that Mr Escome is too old to cope with these strange times and has no one proper to help him. The Parents realize this and they're starting to take their boys away. If you come back, this will stop.

You've had your holiday and time to come to your senses. Now you must start thinking about other people, the people who have cared for you all your life.
Yours ever,
Bessie.

They're still all right for money, he thought. I knew it. So why hasn't Uncle James done what I asked with the rest of mine? And why, *why*, if they're all right for money, couldn't he have had the sense to engage someone decent? They're just not trying. Instead of doing a few very easy things, like finding a proper master, they're just moaning and groaning and writing unnecessary letters, while the boys slip away from under their noses. They don't deserve to be helped. They deserve only silence. And to be silenced.

Still, he thought, this is Bessie's letter, not Georgy's or Uncle James'. I've never liked Bessie: her comments therefore mean nothing to me. If she won't respect my wishes, perhaps *they* will. *They're* the ones who matter, who must realize that I'm now out of their lives. All I want from them is my money. Provided they come across with that and ask nothing of me, all well and good, and never mind what Bessie may say, now or ever. But if Georgy or Uncle James should write in this way, if they too refuse to leave me alone, then I shall have to think again.

But the sum of what Hugo had from James and Georgiana was a brief note from James, in which he said that he hoped Hugo was well and happy and that £1,500, the balance of Hugo's capital, had been paid into his banking account. There was no reference to his return.

What Hugo did not know was that his so called capital did not exist. The money left in trust by his parents was much less than he had been allowed to suppose and had been exhausted long before he went up to Cambridge. This was a secret known only to Lionel and James, who had conspired to prevent Hugo knowing that he was their dependent and to gladden him with the thought that a small but useful sum would one day come to him. It had seemed to them that they could well afford this generosity; but as things had come about, it had been difficult for James to find even the £500 which Hugo had wanted in June, and he would now have 'had no money to give him at all had it not been for Bessie's loan. Of this, about £400 had been spent on the needs of the school, so that nearly all the balance was now absorbed by Hugo. Georgy and Bessie, who still thought Hugo had his own money, did not know this; only the sad old man at Baron's Lodge, confused by drink, tormented by opposing loyalties, knew that the last of his reserves had gone to the distant nephew whom he loved as a second son.

VIII

In the tennis courts at Lord's the galleries lent a Tudor aspect to the murky afternoon. Nigel, watchful among the Hazards, cut the ball back over the net with a quick vicious chop of his racket.

"Chase better than half a yard," called the marker. "Two chases to be wrangled, gentlemen. Change ends."

When they both reached the net, Nigel and his opponent paused to talk.

"He has just arrived," Nigel said, "he's watching in the dedans."

His opponent, who was elderly, emitted a wheeze of satisfaction. "Meaning everything's in order?" he said, with an anxious leer.

"Yes."

"Shall we call it a day then?"

"Seems a pity not to finish the set," Nigel said.

"I've got to save my energies."

"Very well."

They left the court and moved away down a corridor.

"When you're ready," Nigel said, "you will find him in the picture gallery. He will probably be looking at the portrait of Alfred Mynn, for whom, being a man of Kent, he has great affection. He will take you where you need to go."

"Thanks, Nigel. And the – er – ?"

"Money? You'll need a hundred. Cash."

"A hundred?"

"Celebrations of this kind are expensive."

"And your cut?" said Nigel's opponent with a malicious twirl of his racket.

"All you need do is go with the guide and take a hundred pounds with you," said Nigel evenly. Then they were greeted by a poker-faced valet, who showed them to separate bathrooms.

"So far, so good," said Nancy.

"Money up?" asked Hugo.

"A penny or two. But what I meant was that people are being responsive. Word is spreading. And arrangements are actually working."

"Did you ever expect them not to?"

"One is always nervous when starting something new," said Nancy.

"There's nothing very new, my dear, about what we're engaged in."

"It's a new departure for all of us…"

The telephone rang.

"Sloane 2340," Nancy said.

A voice babbled at the other end.

"You can hardly blame us for that," Nancy said. "You were warned, you know."

The voice rose in indignation.

"It was not a mere matter of form," replied Nancy. "You were warned, carefully and advisedly, that beyond a certain point it would be wise to exercise restraint."

The voice was now on the verge of hysteria.

"I'm sorry," Nancy remarked coolly, "but there's nothing whatever to be done."

"Trouble?" asked Hugo, when Nancy had hung up.

"No. Just stupidity."

"It sounded as if someone had been half murdered."

"So they might have been if they hadn't had the sense to move out quickly. Unfortunately they left a dissatisfied client behind."

"Could he be a nuisance?"

"No. His position is rather weak… But he's a clear case for the black list. Upsetting the personnel…"

The telephone rang again. Nancy picked up the receiver.

For thirty seconds she listened to some rapid instructions.

"It's Nigel," she said to Hugo. "He wants you to meet him in Harrods'."

"Harrods'?"

"Yes. That hall with the green armchairs. As soon as you can. There's an important order."

In Sloane Square the newsvendors' placards announced trouble in the Near East. Hugo bought a paper which he examined in his taxi. The usual tale: a small island colony wished to throw off the shackles imposed by the Imperialist British. Well, and why not? Hugo thought. Why not just pull out and leave them to clean up their own shit? That's what they say they want. But of course it isn't. They want us to go, yes, but they also want us to leave our money, our equipment and our *savoir-faire* behind, so that they can take the credit for these themselves. And they'll get their way. There will be bluster and then embarrassment, there will be sanctimonious pronouncements by the Americans, and sooner or later the rebels will win their freedom – a freedom, however, which can only be viable if heavily subsidized by the tyrants whom at present they revile. With a sudden surge of loathing for all subject races, Hugo turned to the racing page. In Harrods' Nigel was looking amused.

"It's Henry Jarvis," he explained. "He's decided to give a party at short notice and wants us to find him some entertainers."

"In which department are we to buy them? Perishable foodstuffs?"

"You're not so far out," said Nigel with a grin. "Come with me."

They took the lift up several floors. When the door opened, they were in a long cavern full of carpets.

"I just want to check up on a friend who works here," Nigel said. "And to introduce you. Take a good look so that you'll know him again."

They moved without sound between the bales of carpet. At length they came to a pile of Persian rugs, behind which was lurking a dapper little youth with a huge quiff of rippling hair above his forehead. When he saw Nigel he grinned amicably.

" 'Lo, dear," he said.

"Good morning, Ronnie," said Nigel politely. "I wondered whether you and Mavis would like to oblige at a party tonight? Short notice but top money."

"Anything you say, dear. We've got nothing on tonight."

"Right. Ring up the Hyde Park Hotel at one fifteen sharp. Ask for the Grill Room and then ask for me by name. I will then confirm the booking, and tell you where to be and when."

"Right-y-oh, Nigel. Thanks. Mave was just saying she hoped we'd be hearing from you."

"Give her my love… And this, Ronnie, is my friend, Hugo Warren. I want you to remember him."

Hugo and Ronnie eyed each other.

"That won't be hard," said Ronnie with a giggle. "Smashing."

Hugo winced.

"All right?" said Nigel.

"All right," said Hugo and Ronnie.

Nigel and Hugo took the lift down again and walked into the street. To judge from the placards at Knightsbridge station the situation in the Near East had deteriorated even during the brief time they had been in Harrods'.

"Santa Kytherea," said Nigel reflectively. "Have you ever been there?"

"No."

"A perfectly foul little island. Nothing but pumice stone and Catholic priests. We shall be well rid of it."

"That's what I thought. Why don't we just pack up and leave?"

"Obstinacy. A few important vested interests."

Nigel stopped and bought a paper.

"Worse and worse," he said. "They're going to reinforce the garrison. *Treble* it, if you please. They don't want another Cyprus, they say."

"Then they know what to do. Get out."

"It's a lesson they can't learn… The Tennis Court at Lord's again this afternoon, Hugo. Be there at four sharp. It's all lined up for poor old Burgo?"

"Just as before. But a different place."

"Good. See you at Lord's. I'm off to settle details with Henry Jarvis."

With a gay wave of the hand, Nigel disappeared into the Hyde Park Hotel.

"Here, you," snarled Gleason at a boy in the front row.

"Yes?" the boy snarled back.

"You know where my room is?"

"Yes."

"Well go there and bring me back a packet of cigarettes. You'll find them in the top left-hand drawer of the chest."

"Which chest?"

"There's only one bloody chest."

"I see, *sir*." The boy got up and slouched out.

"Now," said Gleason, "which of you little perishers can remember what we're meant to be on today?"

Nobody answered. Two boys took out detective novels and started reading them; the rest stared at Gleason with boredom and contempt while he fumbled through a textbook.

"This'll do," he said. "Consecutive clauses: ὥστε with the infinitive. Page 153. Read what the book says, then do the sentences. I'll look at them later."

There was a knock on the door and James Escome came in.

"Everything all right?" he said. "Just popped in to see how the scholarship Greek was going."

"We're doing ὥστε today," said Gleason, "just started."

"ὥστε, eh? That's the stuff. Always a consecutive sentence in every Syntax paper."

There was another knock, or rather the sound of a kick on the door, and the boy Gleason had sent for his cigarettes slouched in past Gleason's desk, slinging the packet on to it as he went.

"There's your cigarettes," he said.

James Escome turned towards Gleason and seemed about to say something. Then he thought better of it and went over to the messenger, who slammed down the lid of his desk on something he had just put in it and looked guiltily up at James.

"There *are* your cigarettes, *sir*," said James.

The boy, who seemed relieved, merely shrugged.

"Answer me properly, King."

"Answer you what? There's nothing to say."

"Then let's see what you say to this," screamed James Escome, picking up a ruler from the next desk and slashing it across King's cheeks. The defiance left the boy's face, to be replaced by a look of fear and pain, and then, oddly, by a look of sorrow. He dabbed at his cheek with a handkerchief to see if there were blood, then at the tears which were forming in his eyes.

"You've never done that before, sir," he whimpered, "never to any of us."

"I know," mumbled James; his hand trembled and the ruler fell to the floor. "I'm sorry, King. It won't happen again."

He made to put his hand on the boy's shoulder, but King, who had already turned sullen once again, shook it off and leaned away.

"I'm sorry," James said, so sorry. "If only you knew…"

As he shambled out of the room, Gleason grinned savagely.

"Going potty if you ask me," he said. He made a crude mime of someone drinking from a bottle, and a sycophant brayed with laughter at the back of the room. An unhappy boy in spectacles bent his head over his text book.

"That's right, Aristotle," said Gleason, "swot it all up. Then you may get to Cambridge and end up teaching it all to a lot of little buggers like yourself – right back where you started from in Baron's bloody Lodge. If the whole place hasn't fallen down by then."

The boy in spectacles went red but continued with his work. The sycophant brayed again. The two boys with detective stories read on imperturbably, secure in the mental retreats to which a wise instinct had long ago guided them. Gleason lit a cigarette, sat down, and propped his feet on his desk.

"I've told you what to do, so now bloody do it," he said, and opened a sweaty paper-covered volume entitled *The English Governess*.

About the time that the boys at Baron's Lodge were sitting down to their high tea, Hugo deposited Nigel's tennis opponent at an address in Camden Town and drove back through foggy streets to Chester Row. When he arrived there, Nancy put down an evening paper headlined "Bomb Outrage in Santa Kytherea" and said, "Long evening in front of you. Henry Jarvis has asked us to do a chemmy game at his party. You'll have to run the cash desk. So go and put on a black tie, and report back here at seven. And pick up Ronnie and Mavis on the way. They'll be waiting in the private bar of the Admiral Benbow in Hugh Lupus Street."

"How very precise and military, my dear. Shall you be coming?"

"I'll be holding the fort here," said Nancy, in her most masculine style. "Which reminds me. Nigel says you'd better give up those chambers of yours and come and live here in the spare bedroom. He thinks the pace is hotting up. We're going to need everyone on the spot the whole time."

"Perhaps we'd better look around for more staff," said Hugo with a giggle. "Anyway, I'll be glad to move in and sample your home cooking."

"As it happens, I think I could be rather a good cook," said Nancy evenly, "but it's a side of me that Nigel doesn't seem to encourage."

"Odd. I should have thought he was very particular about his meals."

"He has an uncertain appetite," said Nancy.

"Then perhaps I can supply the appreciation you need."

"We'll see. Now go and get ready for this spree of Henry's."

Later on, Hugo and Nigel drove down the Great West Road to Henry Jarvis' house, which was near a village called St Peter's in the Meadow. While Ronnie and Mavis conducted an earnest professional conversation in the back, Nigel briefed Hugo about the evening's gambling.

"All you've got to do is to hand out counters against signed IOUs. The values are marked on the counters, so there's no difficulty there. Then stack each chap's IOUs so that you know how much he's into us for."

"No limit?"

"No. Henry's friends are all very rich, and in any case he's guaranteeing them. But keep an eye open in case anyone tries to trot off without meeting his IOUs. It's the least we can do for Henry."

"Wouldn't it be easier if they gave cheques for their counters in the first place?"

"It would, but the very rich won't do it that way. They have to feel that they're loved and trusted. It they were made to play for money down, they'd feel insulted."

"What do I do with the chaps who come out on top?"

"I'll give you a cheque book. Make out cheques for what they've won and send the cheques over to me for signing... This has come unexpected. The next time it happens I'll have arranged with the bank for you to sign. Save us both trouble."

For two or three minutes Hugo pondered this remark and what it implied. Then he said, "What sort of chap is Henry Jarvis?"

"He's a crumb, as our American friends might say. In any properly organized country he'd have been sent to the gas chamber or the salt mines years ago. He's rich and bored and flabby, over-refined in his pleasures and entirely ignorant of anything else. When he talks of being 'civilized,' as he often does, he just means being elaborately vicious."

"Don't forget he's providing our jam, dear," said Ronnie from the back.

"For a person engaged as you and I are," added Hugo to Nigel, "that was rather a severe little speech."

"I'm not ashamed of the services we provide," said Nigel, "but I'm often disgusted by the people we provide them for. It seems a pity so much talent should be wasted on decaying old men like Henry when there are so many young and beautiful people who must go without."

"The young and the beautiful make their own arrangements. In the nature of things we must expect to serve the old and the unappetizing."

"I don't mind myself," said Mavis, "who I do it for. Ronnie and me, we do our stuff, and I don't care if it's King Farouk who's watching or Tom Merry and his pals, so long as I'm paid fair and square at the end of it."

"Quite right," said Nigel. "Professional detachment... We shall be there, chums in two or three minutes. Ronnie and

Mavis, you'll be taken off somewhere to wait till it's time for your act. Whatever Henry's faults, he isn't mean, so there'll be plenty for you to eat and drink. Don't let it sap your energies. Because Henry has undertaken to pay you a minimum of two hundred, but he might well make it five if you amuse his guests. He's very vain of his reputation as a host… Hugo, you and I count as gentry. We sup with the great ones. I don't have to tell you that you will later need a clear head…"

After lights out, King said to the boys in his dormitory, "I found some of those rubber things I told you about in Greaser's drawer when he sent me for cigarettes."

There were gratified murmurs, and several torches were trained on to King's bed.

"Let's have a look…"

"…Try one on…"

"…Stand up so that we can see properly…"

When King, who was a robust twelve and a half, was at the climax of his exhibition, the light went on and Bessie marched in.

"Take that thing off," she said, "and give it to me." Not without difficulty and embarrassment, King obeyed. "Where did you get it?"

King told her.

"And who told you what it was for?"

"I found a book at home. In the holidays."

"I see," said Bessie equably. "But you'll have plenty of time for that game later on. And you should know by now that young gentlemen don't steal. Now go to sleep, all of you; we've had enough nonsense for one evening."

And with a smile of general benediction she switched off the light and went on her way; for being a wise woman, in her own sphere, as well as a good one, she knew that the less drama she made the less damage would result.

After three hours behind his desk, Hugo had taken about ten thousand pounds' worth of IOUs and written one cheque for three hundred odd in favour of an early leaver. Since he was beginning to be bored, he was glad when Henry Jarvis announced that there would now be an interval during which all present might enjoy an extra special treat. This, as Hugo correctly surmised, was Ronnie and Mavis' act. With rheumy eyes and agitated dewlaps, wheezing and croaking with vicarious quasi-lust, the company watched a complex and rather languid erotic dance which culminated in a cunning act of coitus performed in what had been one of Jennifer Stevens' favourite postures. After this, there was a general issue of caviare and champagne, during the consumption of which several elderly men and women approached Nigel Palairet and came away palpably pleased by his response to their requests.

"There's little harm done, Mr Escome," said Bessie, "but that Gleason must go."

"I don't quite see that," said James. "It was hardly his fault. No one can accuse him of direct corruption."

"If he wanted cigarettes from his room, he should have gone and got them himself."

"Perhaps he should. But it's not a matter for dismissal."

"It is if he leaves what he did where a boy might find them," said Bessie. "It says nothing good about him that he had them there at all."

"I don't know. He's a young man... Perhaps he hoped – "

" – what he hoped is his affair," interposed Georgy sternly. "What resulted is ours. Although I don't like Mr Gleason or anything about him, up till now I should have said he must stay, things being as they are, that he must certainly stay until Christmas. But not after this He has shown that intentionally or not he might contaminate. We have other people's children in our care and that is a thing we cannot for one moment risk."

"Well spoken, love," Bessie said.

"Very well," said James, whose eyes were too tired even to show his desperation, "what do you want me to do?"

"Pay Gleason off," said Bessie, "and find young Hugo."

"You know what I feel about Hugo," mumbled James. "Then try to get someone else," said Georgy; "but pay Gleason off and get him out today."

"And meanwhile what about the teaching?"

"We must do as we can about that. If necessary the teaching must wait. We cannot have this – this infection here a day longer."

"Woman's talk," said James, with some return of spirit.

" 'The teaching must wait', you say. Because of course none of you women really think the teaching matters. All that really matters, you think is the woman's side – the beds and the toothpaste and the baths and the pills. The teaching – well that's just something to amuse the children, including the masters, in the intervals between the really vital occupations of taking cod-liver oil and being fitted for new underclothes. If you women had your way, the boys'd grow up as ignorant as yourselves."

"You've no call to turn on us," Bessie said. "And you know very well that we're talking of more than medicines and such. You may not want your boys ignorant, Mr Escome, but you surely want them innocent?"

"What for?" said James. "They'll have to learn some time." His sudden renewed energy was fading away from him now. "The dirt's coming their way whether you like it or not. What's the use of protecting them?" His voice trailed off to a whisper. "Of keeping them pure for a few weeks longer? It'll get them all in the end."

"I've been here almost as long as you have, Mr Escome. But if Gleason stays, I go."

James looked up at Bessie and chuckled.

"I see no cause for mirth," Bessie said.

"You will in a minute." He was laughing with enjoyment but slight uneasiness; like a child who is amused by what he has done but is not quite sure how it will be received by his elders, so that he laughs the louder to reassure himself and to create what he hopes will be an atmosphere of indulgence.

"You will in a minute," James said again. "Now, you want me to pay Gleason the balance of his term's salary and tell him to go?"

"Aye."

"The balance of his salary is two hundred pounds, less income tax and insurance." He slapped his knees and rocked with laughter. "We haven't *got* two hundred pounds.

We've hardly got twenty. We can't get this terrible contaminator out of the place because we're flat broke." He threw back his head and laughed up at the ceiling with long, gurgling bursts.

"And what happened to all my money?"

At this he only laughed the louder.

"Stop it," screamed Georgiana. "Stop it and answer."

"Hugo had it." He pulled a handkerchief from his pocket and wiped the tears from his eyes. "He thought he had money, and he offered to lend it to me, but he hadn't got a penny. Lionel and I had made it all up. So then, when he wanted some for himself, I had to send him Bessie's. Don't you see how funny it is? We're stuck with Gleason and his dirty little tricks. Stuck with him for good."

"A satisfactory evening," said Nigel Palairet on the way back along the Great West Road. "How much did Henry give you, Ronnie?"

"Four hundred. Two each."

"You made quite an impression. I was able to arrange several engagements for you both – together and separately. I'll let you know the details in the morning."

"So long as the money's safe. And no funny business," Mavis said.

"And what, my dear, do you count as funny business?" Nigel asked.

"Instruments," said Mavis. "I'll cope with men and put up with women, and I'll join in with both men *and* women. But I draw the line at instruments."

"Same here," Ronnie said. "Nonsense is one thing, instruments another."

"You needn't worry. I've taken notes of what is required. I take it, Ronnie, you would have no objection to holding a cricket bat?"

"I never was any good at cricket."

"You don't have to be. You just have to dress the part. To revive memories of someone's long lost summer afternoons."

"How very Proustian," observed Hugo.

"How what?" said Ronnie suspiciously.

"Don't worry, Ronnie. He was paying you a compliment," said Nigel.

Later on, after they had dropped Mavis and Ronnie, Nigel said to Hugo, "You must never make literary or intellectual allusions when talking with people like Ronnie. They think they're being laughed at or got at, and that's the one thing they can't stand."

"I'm sorry. But I was being quite sincere. There was something very poetic in the set-up you described. All those torrid afternoons spent sitting outside the pavilion, waiting for God knows what to happen, with the grasshoppers carolling an invitation to come into the long grass – I quite see that someone wants to relive them. Do you think Ronnie would be a suitable companion?"

"Apparently someone does," said Nigel abruptly. "Tell me, Hugo; you got cheques from all the losers?"

"Yes. Twenty-eight thousand, four hundred and seventy in all. The biggest loser was Lord Heathcote. Seven thousand."

"Heathcote's all right… Though his wife Margaret'll be livid with him. How much did we pay out winners?"

"I sent cheques over to you for signature amounting to twenty-five thousand and forty. Which means we're three thousand, four hundred and thirty up. But supposing one of the losers' cheques bounces?"

"I shall put them all in at ten a.m. tomorrow for immediate clearance. If any of them come back, then I ring up Henry Jarvis, who makes up the amount immediately."

"Would he like that?" Hugo asked.

"Not much. But he won't have to. We weren't dealing with common little crooks from Chelsea or SW7. Those people may not have been nice, but their money at least was genuine."

"What will Henry pay us for introducing Ronnie and Mavis?"

"The same as they got for performing."

"A bit rough on them? After all, they actually do the work."

"You must understand," said Nigel, "that no one can do without the go-between. However rich the client, however talented and willing the performers, neither party will get anywhere without a go-between to bring them together. The go-between is the absolute pre-condition both of pleasure and employment. Indeed, the function is so essential that the ancient Greeks saw fit to settle it on a god."

"On Hermes. But only as a side-line."

"The most marginal office of a god," said Nigel, "can command a substantial fee among mere mortals."

IX

One afternoon a day or two later, when Hugo arrived back in Chester Row after a business luncheon, Nancy said to him, "There are two people upstairs in your room. A man and a woman."

"What do they want?"

"You. Otherwise they were not specific."

In Hugo's room the bed was unmade and there were several pairs of dirty socks strewn on the floor. Georgiana was sitting on a hard chair, over the back of which a pair of evening trousers was carelessly folded; she was sitting well forward in order not to disturb the trousers. Harold was sitting on the bed.

"I'm sorry my room is such a mess," said Hugo, elaborately casual. "Would you like to go out to tea?"

"For the time being we should like to stay here," said Harold. "There are matters for discussion."

"Oh?"

"Yesterday I was rung up by Georgy here, who wanted to know if the college had your address."

"She needn't have asked you. Uncle James knows where to find me."

"She couldn't ask James because she couldn't let him know she was coming."

"You're being very mysterious, Harold."

"Am I?" Harold said. "Anyhow, in view of what Georgy said on the telephone, I told her I would get your address from the college office and meet her in London this morning. We went to those chambers you used to keep, and were directed on here, though the porter was reluctant to help us."

"He was being loyal. I expect he thought you were a dun."

"In which case," said Harold, "he was nearer the mark than you might suppose. Tell him about the money, Georgy."

Georgy rose to her feet and stood squarely in front of Hugo like a sergeant-major confronting a recruit.

"The money Daddy sent wasn't yours," she said, "it wasn't even his. You must give it back."

"For Christ's sake," said Hugo, with a mixture of perplexity and venom. "People have been talking about that bloody trust ever since I can remember."

"Tell him, Georgy," said Harold again.

Georgy told him. When she had finished, Hugo stared at her with pure hatred and said, "What in hell do you think I can do about it? I needed that money for a purpose and now it's tied up."

"Tied up in what?" said Harold.

"In business. I'm a partner with the others in this house."

"Curious premises," said Harold. "Who are these people?"

"The woman you saw downstairs is called Nancy Palairet. She is the wife of Nigel Palairet, who is himself an old boy of Baron's Lodge. He was there about the same time as Lionel, and for a little while with me. So you can see this is all perfectly respectable. Georgy, you must remember him?"

"I remember him," said Georgy. "He was a polite, kind boy. If we told him what has happened, he'd release you and the money, I know he would, unless he's changed."

"You're not to ask him," shouted Hugo. "I mean – you *can't* ask him. He's away."

This was true; Nigel was in Paris and would not be back for three days. But the respite, Hugo reflected, was slender; it was no good bullying; Georgy would have to be cajoled.

"Look, Georgy," he said. "You must realize that I need this money and that morally at least it belongs to me. For years I've been allowed to expect it. When things were hard for Uncle James, I offered him some of it – in good faith, Georgy. And then, when I wanted it for my own purposes, I asked for it and received it – again in good faith. You can't just turn round now and tell me it belongs to Bessie…of all people, to Bessie."

"But it does belong to Bessie, Hugo. And we're desperate for it. I haven't told you yet what else has been happening."

And then, as Hugo listened at first with loathing and then with fury, she told him of James' drinking, of Gleason, of the air of decay and collapse which hung over the school as over a little Byzantium.

"Why can't you cope with your own troubles?" Hugo burst out at last. "I've faced mine and come to terms." He clenched and unclenched his fists, rapidly, time after time. "And now, just when I'm nicely settled, just when things have started to go right, you come whining to me for help and money. It isn't fair." He was almost weeping with self pity. "It simply isn't fair."

"Daddy helped you when you had nowhere to go."

"That debt can't stand for ever. Both your father and Lionel said so."

"Listen. Hugo." Harold leant forward and took him by the wrist. "We're not going to stay here and argue. Legally, we can't get this money from you. Bessie lent it to James and James gave it to you, and the only legal pressure that can be brought is on James to repay Bessie. But you must know what gratitude and decency – decency above all, Hugo – require of you. For your own sake, Hugo, you must give back this money and put yourself at the service of your uncle. Or at least give back the money. If you don't, you're lost."

"I've told you, Palairet has the money. It's no longer mine to give back."

"Georgy seems to think well of Palairet. You must ask him to release it. If you don't, I will. Come along, Georgy."

Georgy and Harold went down the stairs together. White-faced, Hugo stood at the top and watched them go. Then Nancy came out into the hall.

"Mrs Palairet," said Georgy, "I am an old acquaintance of Nigel's. This gentleman and I have business with him. Could you tell us when he will be back?"

Nancy glanced up the stairs at Hugo, who shrugged hopelessly.

"I expect him on Friday afternoon," she said.

"Thank you," said Harold courteously, and opened the door for Georgy to pass into the street.

Nancy started up the stairs towards Hugo.

"You look very put out," she said. "What was all that?"

Hugo looked down at Nancy. He steadied himself against the banister, puckered his forehead reflectively; slowly the colour came back into his face and with it came hope.

"Trouble," Hugo said, "but only for me."

"Tell me."

"You'll know soon enough." He held out his hands and she came on up the stairs.

"Tell me," she repeated. "Perhaps I can help."

"Perhaps you can. But it'll keep awhile."

When he had her hands in his, he drew her right up against him.

"When Nigel left this morning," he said, "I thought to myself, 'This is what I'll do to Nancy if she'll let me...' "

He began to tell her. Calling up all his memories of a summer with Jennifer, he talked to her quietly and fast; and as the last of the December light faded from the windows, he led her to his unmade bed.

"But listen, Hugo," Nancy said. They were dining, that same evening, in a restaurant carefully selected by Hugo to afford space and leisure for conspiracy. "Listen, my darling," she said, "you heard that don-man say that they had no legal claim on the money. So the money can stay with Nigel and you can stay with us."

"He also said he was going to ask Nigel to give it back. You know how Nigel feels about Baron's Lodge. He's been pestering me about it since the day we met."

"But Nigel can't just dispose of *your* money as he thinks fit."

"Possibly not. But this will be the end of me as far as he's concerned."

"I can speak to him."

"No doubt. But you yourself have encouraged him to think that certain masculine loyalties must be beyond the interference of a wife. In this case he won't listen to you. He will act on an earlier love."

"Loyalties," said Nancy, "are important, but they must be seen in a proper context. For example, I have not been disloyal to Nigel by going to bed with you because the bond between Nigel and myself has never been a sexual one. Such as it is, this bond, it remains unaltered by what happened this afternoon."

"Is he impotent then? Or what?"

"I think he finds his outlet in this work we are all doing... But there will be time to talk about him later. I was saying that loyalties are only valid within their proper context. You have been absolved from further duty to Baron's Lodge by your uncle's own words and actions. *He* told you not to come back unless you wanted to: *he* sent you money despite his difficulties: *he* would not have let his daughter come to you had he known. All this sets you free from him."

See how she twists it, he thought, in the interest of her newly-found pleasure; nothing will make her let me go now. Aloud he said, "Nigel won't see it like that. He will say that after all this time there can be no absolution for me. Whatever my uncle says or does."

"We shall find a way of convincing Nigel."

She sought for his hand under the table and crushed it against the inside of her thigh. Just as everything was going so well, he thought; a few months of this and I should have enough money to cut away and do whatever I wished. But no, Georgy and Bessie are whining after my pathetic capital, Harold is putting on George Eliot attitudes about duty, they are all determined to bring me back to their own wretched level. Well, they shan't have me or the money; with this woman, who is ruthless and resourceful, to guide me, I shall be able to ride right over this one obstacle that is left, If necessary, she would clear it with her bare hands from my path.

Next morning, while Nancy was out the telephone rang.

"My name's Culbertson," said a tired voice, "adjutant of the Eleventh Battalion of the Sixth or Carbinier Guards. Speaking from Windsor."

"I didn't know the Carbiniers had eleven battalions," said Hugo.

"We don't. The Eleventh Battalion is just the name we use for a special force made up of Territorials and Reservists. But I don't know why I'm telling you all this. I want to speak to Captain Palairet. NHS Palairet. Nigel. Is he there?"

"No. Can I help you?"

"Well the thing is this. The Eleventh Battalion is forming to go to Santa Kytherea. I've got Nigel down on the roll as a Reservist of the First Class. Which means we can call on him without notice if we need him. Naturally," said the voice more tiredly than ever, "we don't want to bother him if he's got anything important on, and we wouldn't dream of using our powers in the matter. Never do. But if he'd like to come we'd be particularly glad to have him, because someone here says he knows the island."

"He does."

"Ah. Thank God someone's got something right for once. But since I don't know who you are, Mr – er – ?"

"Warren. Hugo Warren."

" – Mr Warren, I really think I've told you enough. Where can I find Nigel?"

"His wife may know but she's out. When did you want him?"

"Sooner the better. The battalion doesn't leave for some days, but we've got Nigel provisionally booked for Intelligence Officer, so we'd be sending him on ahead with the advance party to have a look round. Tomorrow, that is. Or so they tell me. But I'm not at all sure I ought to be discussing it with you."

"I'm an old friend of Nigel's. If you like, I'll try and get hold of him. As I say, his wife may be able to help."

"That's very civil of you, Mr...er. Tell him not to worry if he can't make it but some of the chaps would be glad to see him again. And I'd better give you our telephone number, if I can find out what it is. Only got here yesterday myself, you see. Sergeant-Major... Of course. Written on the bloody thing. Windsor 55555, extension Omega. I know it sounds odd, but they're using Greek letters for the confidential line."

"Are you sure you ought to be telling me that?"

"So long as you're an old chum of Nigel's... Tell me, your number, Sloane 2340, it seems sort of familiar. Fellow I know was saying only the other day that if one wanted... But I expect I've got it mixed up..."

"I expect so," said Hugo. "I'll see what I can do about Nigel for you."

After he had rung off he consulted a diary on Nancy's desk. Twenty minutes later he was through to Nigel in Paris.

"Advance party, you say? Tomorrow?"

"That's it."

"It's no good, Hugo. I'm up to my ears here, and in any case I can't leave England for weeks or months at this stage in affairs. Ring up Willie Culbertson at Windsor and tell him it's not on."

"He said that as a Reservist of the First Class you were bound to come when called."

"But he knows perfectly well that there's a gentleman's agreement about this. When we all joined, the colonel promised that anyone who was heavily committed at home would not be pressed."

"Culbertson said they were desperate for an intelligence officer who knew Santa Kytherea. I said you were very busy, and he said 'Doing what?' and so then it was a little difficult to explain."

"Look, Hugo. I hate doing this, but you'll have to ring up Willie and tell him you can't find me. I can't go off to war with things as they are."

"Culbertson also said there were a lot of old friends looking forward to seeing you."

For twenty seconds there was complete silence on the line.

"Nigel? Are you all right?"

"No. Now listen carefully, Hugo. I'll do what I can here and catch the lunchtime plane. Meanwhile, get hold of Nancy and make sure she's in Chester Row at three p.m. sharp to discuss arrangements with me. It may take us some time. I'll go straight from the plane to the bank and then come on to Nancy in Chester Row…"

At Baron's Lodge the radiators went from hot to lukewarm to dead cold. The boys, pinched and shivering, did not even pretend to do their work. Gleason shrugged his shoulders and sent a boy to his room for a blanket, which he draped about himself like a shawl. Georgy sought out Bessie.

"They won't send any more coal till the bill's paid."

"What are you going to do, love?"

"Nigel Palairet's due back the day after tomorrow. Harold and I will be waiting for him in London. Meanwhile, I want you to make Daddy go to bed and stay there."

"And the boys?"

"They'll just have to put up with it. We'll say the heating system has gone wrong. There are no parents coming till Sunday, and by then everything should be all right."

"Now look here, Willie," said Nigel in Culbertson's office that evening. "I want to know why I've been forced to come here. You know the agreement as well as I do."

"There's no question of forcing you to come, old man. I just told this chap – what's his name? – "

" – Warren – "

" – Yes, Warren – I just told him on the telephone we'd be glad to see you and we wanted someone who'd been to this beastly island. But if you had anything important on, I said, not to worry."

'That's not at all what he told me."

"He must have got it mixed up. Not to worry, I said, if you couldn't make it."

"I see," said Nigel. "So I'm not being pressed?"

"Course not. You know better than that."

"In that case, Willie, I'm not coming. I'm starting up something new and I can't leave it now. Nancy would have done her best, but if I don't *have* to go with you, then it's a thousand times better I should stay and do it myself. You do understand?"

"Course I do, old man. I said so all along. I can't imagine what that fellow Warren thought he was doing."

"I think I can."

"Well, it's no affair of mine," said Culbertson. "Come and have a drink. Have some dinner and stay the night. You can run back in the morning."

"I ought to get back as soon as possible."

"Just one drink, old man. They'll all be in the Mess. Been looking forward to seeing you, too."

"Just one drink then."

When they entered the Mess, five or six figures rose from odd corners and drifted towards Nigel in front of the fireplace.

"Hallo, Nigel, wondered when you'd arrive…"

"Have a drink, old chap. Ring the bell, Reresby, if you've got enough strength…"

"Nice to see you, Nigel. Alastair was just saying he was wondering when you'd show up."

"Hallo, Eddie," said Nigel, "…Reresby… Alastair… Hallo, Charles… Iain."

"That'll be four whiskies, Corporal, and three pink gins. Good thing you got there when you did, Nigel. We were beginning to think you might be tied up. You'd have been missed, old man."

"That's right. Wouldn't have been at all the same without you. Iain was just saying, a few minutes before you came in…"

"I suppose," said Nigel Palairet to Willie Culbertson, "I shall need battledress or something before leaving with the advance party tomorrow? I've only got my old SD."

"That'll be all right," said Culbertson. "They'll fit you out in Santa. What's it's name. Sure Nancy's going to be all right? And that Warren fellow?"

"I don't know," said Nigel. "I shall find out when I get back. Here's luck, Eddie and Charles… Alastair, Reresby… Iain…"

"So that's it," said Nancy to Hugo, tapping a list in front of her. "These are engagements already booked with notes about what we must do to keep them. And this," she took a second sheet from a drawer, "is a list of various types of contact. We're going to have our work cut out."

"Any more gambling parties?"

"No. Nigel suggests we only run those if someone like Henry Jarvis asks us – that we don't get up anything on our own."

"They could be profitable," said Hugo thoughtfully.

"Nigel's idea is that we should keep things ticking over till he gets back rather than look for extra profit. But if there were to be gambling, you'd have to do croupier. Could you cope?"

"I watched Nigel for a time the other night. I think so. And you'd sit demurely there at the cash desk?"

"I suppose so. And that's another thing. Control of money."

"Ah?"

"When we started there was £9,000 in the account – £ 7,500 of Nigel's and £1,500 of yours. Now, what with one thing and the other, it's nearer £15,000. Which means a profit, after just under a month, of £6,000; your share being £ 1,000 – a sixth of the profit as you put up a sixth of the capital."

"Equitable."

"Now, Nigel has given me complete control of the account for the duration of his absence. He told me he had been meaning to empower you to sign cheques for certain purposes, and suggested I should now do so."

"Oh?" said Hugo.

Nancy got up and walked towards him. She put her hands round his waist and rubbed herself against his body.

"But I'm not going to," Nancy said, "because I don't trust you."

"I beg your pardon?"

"I want you here, I adore you, but I don't trust you. Besides, Nigel rang me up from Windsor last night."

"What's that got to do with it?"

"On the face of it, nothing. He said he was leaving with the advance party this morning."

"Well then?"

"But he also told me to give you his love. There was something odd about the way he said it."

"You're imagining things," Hugo said.

"No. I've got a good instinct. What was it he said? 'Give Hugo my love, and thank him for getting hold of me so promptly.' It sounded as if he thinks you're glad he's out of the way."

"So I am, if I can have you to myself."

"There's more to it than that. You're expert with me but not loving. Anyone would do as well as me – I know that. So I'm holding on to the purse strings, my love."

"If Nigel had wanted you to do that, he'd have said so on the telephone."

"Not necessarily. He's very fond of you. Even if he thought you were disloyal, he wouldn't say so to anyone else until all possible doubt were gone. Anyhow, it's your little Nancy, my darling Hugo, who wants to hold on to the purse strings, and that's what she's going to do."

She lowered her hands from his waist and scratched his buttocks with her fingernails.

"You're learning fast," said Hugo. "It will be a pleasure to instruct you further… Incidentally, had it occurred to you that with Nigel out of the way, no one will be able to make trouble about Baron's Lodge. Even if they write to him, he won't be able to pick an effective quarrel with me all the way from Santa Kytherea. And he can hardly hand over my money to them without my permission. If he gives them £1,500, it'll be his own."

"What a rat you are," said Nancy softly, digging into his flesh with her nails.

"I thought you were on my side about Baron's Lodge."

"I am. But you're so calculating about it. Adding up to the last little detail… What are you going to do when your cousin and that don-man come to see Nigel? If you like," she said lightly, "I'll pay them that £1,500. You'd still have £1,000 invested; so you'd still get about a twelfth of the profits."

"I owe them *nothing*," scowled Hugo. "If they can't manage for themselves, then they must go under."

"But what shall you say to them?"

"I shan't be here. You must tell them that Nigel's gone and then get rid of them."

"You're afraid."

"Only of one thing," Hugo said. "If I were to see that pale, virtuous, pleading face of my cousin's just once more, I should be tempted to kill her."

"My husband has gone with his reserve unit to Santa Kytherea," said Nancy on Friday afternoon. "I don't know when he'll be back."

"His address?" said Harold shortly.

"He said he'd write later and let me know. He left in rather a hurry."

"You know why we're here?" said Georgiana.

"No," said Nancy dismissively.

"My cousin Hugo had placed money with your husband that does not belong to him."

"I am handling my husband's affairs while he is away. If you have proof of this, I shall be glad to set the matter right."

"There's no actual proof," said Harold, "but Hugo knows it to be so."

"Then as soon as Hugo tells me to, I will release the money."

"Where *is* Hugo?" said Georgy. "Where *is* he?"

"He is away," said Nancy, "he has gone on business to Brussels." She rose to her feet. "When he gets back, I will tell him that you came."

"So what now, love?" Bessie said.

"Harold had a little money put by. Enough to pay Gleason and the rest the balance of their salaries for the term. Enough to settle some of last month's bills."

"So at least we can have some heat, love?"

"Not until after the weekend. I paid the coal people this morning. They said that today was Saturday and they couldn't, or wouldn't, deliver before Monday."

116

"There's parents coming Sunday."

"I know… Daddy has had more withdrawals, Bessie. Seven. The word's getting out that things are…wrong with us."

"At least you can now sack Gleason," Bessie said. "That's one wrong put right."

"But is it? What sort of offer can we make to anyone else? I don't know what to do, Bessie. I've even thought of sending them all home. Saying there's scarlet fever or something. Shall I, Bessie? Shall I?"

"No, love. They'd find you out in the lie."

"You're right, of course… What do you make of Daddy?"

"I've been giving him pills to make him rest. But he can't lie in bed for ever."

"Till Monday. We don't want the parents to see him."

Sunday was a day of gales along the coast of Kent. Parents, disagreeably disposed after long December drives, saw frozen, dirty boys huddled together in whispering groups. Four of them, having demanded to see James and been told that he was ill, asked Georgiana, with scant politeness, to see that their boys' trunks were packed by the evening, when the boys would be taken away for good. By Monday afternoon the radiators were working again; the warmth they gave could bring little comfort to Baron's Lodge.

X

Christmas was an active season for Nancy and Hugo. Many of their regular clients were away, but those that weren't seemed depressed by the festival and the more anxious in consequence to avail themselves of the consolations which were so efficiently dispensed from Chester Row. In the intervals of business Hugo made love to Nancy with assiduity and precision, introducing all the refinements which he had investigated with Jennifer the previous summer.

From Baron's Lodge they heard nothing. From Nigel there were several long letters which combined business suggestions with rather troubled accounts of what was to do in Santa Kytherea. It appeared that the early outrages there had ceased; and that, although there was daily and public agitation of a more or less legal kind, actual hostilities had been suspended while the nationalists considered the new problems presented by the reinforcement of British troops in the island. It was thought that militant opposition to the British was being established underground; but since the intelligence services were skeletal and inept, they had nothing to offer beyond this general proposition, which was in any case almost tautologous. As for Nigel's battalion, it merely sat about like all the others in an uneasy state of readiness for some unspecified type of disaster, a vile condition of service which was somewhat improved by the pleasing features of the little harbour town of Port Orestes which was central to its area. But although the

officers contrived to be content, the rank and file, inimical to
foreign food and customs, conscious of families left at home and
ungenerous allowances paid to them, and piqued, as the days of
inaction passed, by their own apparent redundance, became
resentful and then almost mutinous. It was, Nigel wrote, a
disagreeable situation (despite the brisk and palatable local
wines), and he could only hope that something, anything,
would happen before the battalion should be overwhelmed by
atrophy or hysteria.

"They may stay there for years," Hugo said to Nancy, "or
they may come home tomorrow. My bet is that if nothing
happens they'll replace all reservist units within a month of
their leaving England. The families will start whining and the
politicians will get windy."

"And if something does happen?"

"Then they'll be committed. They'll have to see it through.
Do you hope something will happen, Nancy?"

"I don't know. I'm happy with you, yet I want Nigel back
safe. So far, I've managed to convince myself that it's much the
same as if he were just away on manoeuvres. But if it gets to be
like it was in Cyprus…"

"Not many were killed there. And Nigel's got a nice, safe job.
I think we shall get on very well without him for a bit."

"I want him back, Hugo."

"When he's back, there'll be an end of this." He leant over
her, as she sat at her desk, and cupped her breasts in his hands.

"What a swine you are." As he fondled her her whole body
tensed and her thighs began to straddle.

"Anyhow," said Hugo casually, but at the same time putting
all his skill into his caresses, "there's nothing we can do about
it."

Nancy got to her feet and started half pulling him and half
coaxing him towards the door.

"Come on," she said, "come on, my darling, come on."

"One little matter first."

"Later," she said, "come on, please come on."

"Now. Henry Jarvis wants me to run another chemmy game for him. On New Year's Eve. You'll be busy that night. You must authorize me to sign the cheques."

"Oh God," She turned to face him. "No. You know what I said about that. No."

As she stood there trembling, he started to undo the buttons of her dress. He put his hand inside for a few seconds, then withdrew it and stood back.

"You must," he said, "we can't disappoint Henry."

"No, no, we won't. I'll come with you and do the cheques. I'll change that other arrangement, they don't need me really, I was only going to bring them together and show them – "

She came at him with dress and arms open.

" – We can't go changing arrangements," he said as he stepped farther away, "it's unprofessional. You must keep your appointment, and I must go to Henry's authorized to handle the money."

He came back towards her and put his hand inside her dress once more.

"That's right, isn't it?" he said. "I must be properly authorized, mustn't I?"

"Yes, yes," she almost shouted at him, "yes, yes, anything you say, but *for Christ's sake don't stop now.*"

A day or two after Christmas James Escome summoned Georgy and Bessie to his study. He was relaxed and unquestionably sober.

"Since the summer," he said calmly, "thirty boys have been withdrawn, many of them only a week or so ago. There will be more. We can't carry on."

"But Mr Escome," Bessie began.

James held up his hand.

"We can't keep Gleason," he said. "I see that now. Never mind that wretched business over King. The point is that he knows nothing and has taught nothing. The end of term exams were a mere farce, but I could just gather that."

"We can get someone else," Georgy said.

"We could afford another Gleason," James replied. "We could struggle on with the fees due for next term. But we have nothing left to offer. It would be a mockery, a fraud. The spirit has gone, you see. Lionel took it with him. Perhaps Hugo might have – " He checked himself. "But he hasn't, and now he won't. I'm going to write to all the parents and tell them we must close. They'll have to place their boys as best they can during the next three weeks, but anywhere, or nowhere would now be better than here."

"What about the young masters? They'll expect notice."

"I've written to them explaining the position. I've given them all good references, and promised to pay them a term's salary when and as the means become available."

"Means?" said Bessie. "What means can there ever be without the fees?"

"There is a little money to come," said James, "from last term's arrears and extras. The three of us can live on that for the time. If either of you wish to leave, I shall quite understand; there is, after all, no future here. Equally, I shall be happy if you care to stay and keep me company."

"But how are we to *exist*, Daddy? The arrears, the extras…even if everyone pays promptly, it's almost nothing."

James turned down his eyes.

"I was talking to Hunt the draper at the golf club dinner," he said. "As you know, Mrs Hunt is now Councillor, and he has heard that the Council is anxious for another housing estate up here. He told me straight out that if I needed money he knew they would buy our games' field. His wife, in particular, is keen this should happen. It would be her final revenge on us, you see, to wall us up with council houses."

"Did Mr Hunt say that?"

"Not in so many words. He seemed distressed. He wanted, I think, to help us."

"But Daddy, our beautiful field...after all these years of cricket..."

Again James held up his hand.

"I know how you feel, my dear. But there will not be much more cricket now at Baron's Lodge."

"The bank passes," Hugo said, "at a thousand pounds. What offers?"

"Five hundred," said a man with a face as bland as a Dutch cheese.

"Six."

"Seven."

"Eight," said the Dutch cheese.

"Nine."

"One thou' then," said the Dutch cheese affably, "someone should have said so in the first place."

"Bank to Lord Heathcote at a thousand," Hugo said.

"Banco," said a man with cheeks like unripe gorgonzola. Heathcote flicked a card out of the shoe for his opponent, then one for himself, then repeated the process. The gorgonzola consulted its cards and announced that it would stand. Heathcote then turned up his cards, an eight and a ten.

"Natural eight for the bank," called Hugo.

The gorgonzola, his blue veins now red with annoyance, huffily pushed over a pile of blue plaques, each marked £100. Hugo changed one of these for two red plaques marked £50 and put one of the latter in a slotted box by his right hand.

"House takes fifty," he said. "Does the bank wish to make up a round figure?"

The Dutch cheese gave a kind of wobble and a red plaque landed in the centre of the table.

"Two thousand pounds in the bank," called Hugo.

"*Banco suivi*," said the gorgonzola tightly.

The hand was played. This time the gorgonzola turned up a natural eight but Lord Heathcote produced a nine. The gorgonzola's veins flickered violently, like a neon light being switched on.

"Bank wins with a natural of nine," Hugo said. He took a blue plaque for his box. "Five per cent for the house is one ton. Thank you, sir," this to the gorgonzola, who had just produced two white plaques, which resembled miniature tomb stones and were worth a thousand pounds each, to pay his losses.

"Give me another five thousand," said the gorgonzola crossly.

That'll be twenty thousand he owes on the book, Hugo thought. He managed to catch Henry Jarvis' eye, for Jarvis, after all, would be responsible if things went wrong. But Jarvis only gave a barely perceptible nod, which clearly meant "Don't be so impertinent as to question my guests." All right, Hugo thought; it's your party. He wrote a figure on the paper beside him, then handed the gorgonzola three plaques for a thousand, two for five hundred, and ten for one hundred. The gorgonzola, who was superstitious as well as mean, tossed one of the hundreds back.

"*Pour les employés*," he said, "may bring me luck."

Hugo bowed.

"*Merci, m'sieur, pour les employés*," he called, "and now, gentlemen, there are four thousand in the bank…"

The play that night was high. At the end of the evening, Hugo had to write cheques for nearly seventy thousand pounds, against which he received cheques for eighty-four thousand pounds, payable, as was customary in these circles, to Cash. Of these cheques, he paid in eighty-one thousand pounds' worth, asking that immediate clearance be effected, the next morning at Nigel's bank; two cheques, which totalled just under three thousand, he paid into his own. For as he surmised, Nancy would hardly question a profit in a single evening of eleven thousand, and, when all was said, it was himself that had done the work.

Nigel Palairet and Willie Culbertson drank ouzo and watched the sun as it sank behind the mountains on the other side of the bay.

"News this morning," Culbertson said.

"Oh?"

"If nothing happens within the next week, we're going home."

"Not before time," said Nigel. "It's as much as I can do to keep the ten men of my intelligence section in order. Heaven help the Company commanders."

"I'd have thought," said Willie, "that the intelligence section at least would have had something to do. Don't Brigade tell you anything?"

"Brigade don't know anything. No one does. The Army Intelligence set-up works as smoothly as a muzzle-loading cannon, and the local agents are too scared to be any help. But of course it's obvious what will happen."

"What?"

"The same as has happened everywhere else. The nationalists will establish themselves in the mountains. When they're ready, they'll come skipping down for a series of hit and run raids, and then go back into hiding."

"Then why aren't we searching the mountains?" said Culbertson. "Digging them out before they get settled?"

"Because such a search would constitute 'aggression'. We're on the wrong side, Willie; we're fighting the times. These days, people who want independence are 'right', however unpleasant the methods they use to get it, and those who try to prevent them are 'wrong' – no matter how sensible their reasons or how scrupulous their conduct. And right or wrong, we can't win; the Government will give way to the nationalists in the end, as it always has. But as a matter of face it can't give in straight away.

The political *convenances* require a delay of between eighteen months and three years, and we're here to secure it."

"But you've just said there's nothing we can do even now we are here. It would be called 'aggression', you said."

"We can clear up the mess, Willie. We can't do anything until real trouble starts, we can't do much when it *does* start, but in the intervals between trouble we can wash the blood off the streets and tidy away the dead. Make believe everything's normal again – until the next time."

"Bleak look-out."

"Worse. The army in Santa Kytherea is a sort of punching bag. We're here to amuse the terrorists, to give them a large and well-defined target to take pot shots at, so that they don't start on the officials and politicians who are actually responsible for the delay. We're here to draw off the bullets, Willie, and no one will encourage us to shoot back."

"But surely, old man, they must just let us defend ourselves, whatever else we mustn't do."

"Not a bit of it. You see, if we *do* shoot back, we might frighten the enemy, who will then decide that officials and politicians would be easier game. You remember what happened in Cyprus? The army came out on top once or twice, and then the young heroes of EOKA got so shit-scared of taking on anything in uniform that they started killing civilians. They won't want that here, so they'll probably come up with some formula forbidding 'premature' self-defence – meaning that you can't fire back until half your men are dead and you've got two doctors to sign the death certificates."

Willie looked depressed and ordered another two ouzos.

"Then the only hope," he said, "is to get out before anything happens?"

"That's it, Willie. The men know it too, which is why they're so restless... A week, you said? If nothing happens in a week, they'll send us home?"

"So I'm told, old man."

"Well," said Nigel, "here's to peace for another week." He reached for his glass and raised it towards the mountains.

The Council was prompt with its offer to James. There was to be a new factory in the district, new accommodation was needed, and the cricket field at Baron's Lodge was worth fifty thousand pounds as a municipal building site (about half the sum, though James was not to know this, which a private contractor would have offered). The bank manager, his rodent eyes now rendered unctuous, advised James to accept.

"But if the land is worth so much," said James thoughtfully, "why did you refuse me a loan last summer?"

"That was different, Mr Escome. So long as you were only going to use it for small boys to play cricket on it was worth nothing. But now it's to be put to a proper purpose… I take it you will wish us to invest the money for you? Even in the safest stock it should yield two thousand a year."

"Yes," said James, "you invest it when it comes. But keep five thousand handy in cash. If things have got to end this way, one may as well have a little fun."

"As you direct," said the bank manager disapprovingly. Nevertheless, he showed James out with a bow.

Funny, thought James; first time in my life with nothing to do all day. Even in the holidays there was always plenty to arrange. In the summer there'll be cricket to watch, but it's some time to go before the summer. Perhaps Georgy and Bessie would like a little trip abroad. We all need a bit of a break. I don't really know where to go, though, not at this time of the year. Hugo would have known; he always knew about that kind of thing. I wish Hugo were here; then I could ask him about it and perhaps he'd even come with us. I wish he'd come to see us. All these months, I've wished that he might come – not to stay, if he didn't want to, but just to see us. But I don't suppose he'll come again. Not now.

"Baron Lazlo wants Ronnie and Mavis for the ninth," Nancy said.

Hugo went to Harrods' to find Ronnie.

"Sorry, dear," said Ronnie. "Mavis is not well."

"But, Ronnie... Think of the money."

"It makes me want to cry, dear. But Mav's still not well. Measles. All over everywhere. You do see?"

Hugo went back to Chester Row.

"There's a possible thousand in it," he told Nancy. "Up to five hundred for the turn itself and the same again for the introduction."

"Pity," Nancy said, "but we can do without."

"Besides," Hugo went on, "it'll be bad for our reputation if we let Lazlo down."

"It can't be helped. Even people as rich as Lazlo can't always have their own way."

"Nancy. It would be very easy to keep Lazlo happy and collect the whole thousand for ourselves."

At first she didn't understand him. Then she smacked him hard across the chops.

"You'd do that to me," she said, her tone rapidly subsiding from anger to sorrow, "for a miserable thousand pounds?"

"We're not so rich we can sniff at a thousand pounds. Besides, it'll be a new experience, it might even be rather fun. You can wear a mask if you're shy. We can't run to a dance, of course, but we should be able to work out quite a jolly routine."

"But the *shame* – "

"You have always disavowed moral shame. You do not seem to me conspicuous for sexual shame. Why talk of shame now?"

"Social shame," said Nancy, looking at the ground.

"So now you're being snobbish? Come off it, dear. This lot may accept Nigel, but they don't give a damn for you or me. You must have seen in their faces. We're just – " he hesitated, then called up a phrase of Lionel's from long ago – "we're just

127

a species of upper servant as far as they're concerned. We may just as well drop all pretences and take their money."

"No, Hugo. I can't do it. And suppose Nigel heard?"

"You owe Nigel no sexual loyalty. You said so yourself."

"I know. But *this...*"

"*This* is an office which has not been disdained by empresses. You'll do what I say," said Hugo affably, "or you'll regret it very much. We can't let a thousand quid go begging." He put his hand across to where Nancy was sitting, let it linger awhile, then withdrew it abruptly. "You see what I mean?"

"You're horrible. You know that I should...half die, if you...went away from me..."

"I never pretended to be nice," Hugo said. "And since you've grasped my point so thoroughly, we may as well start rehearsing our appearance now. Or would you sooner wait till tomorrow?"

Two days before Nigel's battalion was to be relieved, a supply depot was raided at the other end of the island.

"That does it," said Willie Culbertson. "Anything can happen now. And even if it doesn't, they won't let us go."

"I must say," said Nigel, "I was praying we'd get out in time. I'm beginning to worry about Nancy. Her letters are odd..."

"Me too. Fiona's going frantic. And to make things worse," said Willie, "she's got to find a new school for Nicholas. Old one's closing down, just like that. One of the best in the country, too – Baron's Lodge."

"What's that?" said Nigel, gripping Culbertson's arm with both hands as though it alone kept him from the abyss.

"Steady on, old chap. I said Nickie's school's closing down. Not that the end of the world had come."

"Baron's Lodge. I was there, Willie."

"Well, you know what it is, old man. These prep. schools, they sprout up and then shrivel away like mushrooms. They have scandals, they change hands, they go bust. None of them lasts more than twenty years, and in most cases it's against the public interest they should last two."

"Baron's Lodge wasn't that kind of school."

"But apparently it was, old man," said Willie.

"What happened?"

"Usual sort of story. Old man's son died, things started to go wrong, went from bad to worse, duns all over the bloody place, so they decided to sell up."

"Sell up? Baron's Lodge?"

"Something of the sort. Fiona's not too clear about the details. She did say the old man had been drinking. Typical of her to find that out. Bloody, inquisitive bitch," said Willie cheerfully.

"James Escome? Drinking?"

"You seem to have a pretty rosy view of the place. Must say, I always liked the look of it myself."

"Why didn't Hugo – ?"

"What's that?"

"Nothing. Look, Willie. If I pay my own passage, can I go home? Compassionate leave?"

"If you've got good grounds."

"I want to help them at Baron's Lodge."

"Too late, old man. Place is closed. Anyhow, you'd look a bit of a fool telling Colonel Guy you wanted to go home because your old prep. school had gone to buggery – just now, when the shooting's going to start. I think," said Willie, with something of an edge to his voice, "that you'd better stay here with the rest of us."

As Hugo had hoped, the novel circumstances at Baron Lazlo's, so far from inhibiting Nancy, aroused her to a screaming frenzy. Their efforts were much applauded, and Baron Lazlo showed his appreciation with a most generous cheque.

A few nights later, Hugo again ran a chemmy game. This time the profit from the house percentages was just over seven thousand pounds, of which Hugo took three thousand for himself. When Nancy commented that their takings were much smaller than on the previous occasion, Hugo told her, with some truth, that the game had been lower and the turnover therefore much less.

James wrote to Hugo from Baron's Lodge.

...So what with one thing and another, I've decided to give up. It seems that the sale of the field will fetch enough for us to live comfortably, so for the time being we shall stay at the old place. At least, Georgy and I shall. I don't yet know what Bessie's going to do, though of course she knows she can stay here as long as she likes.

We've missed you, my dear boy, over the last few months, but we all realized that you had a lot to attend to, starting from scratch in London. What exactly is it you do, by the way? Anyhow, perhaps you've settled down well enough by now to afford a few days off. If so, we'd be very happy to see you. It seems such a long time, and it would be splendid to hear all your news.

My love as ever,

James

PS The men came to dismantle the cricket pavilion the other day; but I decided to keep those boards Lionel did with the names of the XIs – you remember, I expect – in red and gold. Although there's no use for them now, it seemed a pity so much work should just go up in smoke.

J

Hugo read through his uncle's letter with care; then he tore it across and across, until the scraps of paper dribbled through his fingers like confetti.

And so Nigel Palairet, puzzled and sad, drank ouzo underneath the mountains and waited for what they must now at any moment bring forth. James Escome pottered over the field that would soon belong to others, remembering many afternoons he had passed on it and waiting for a letter from Hugo which he knew in his heart, would never come; while Hugo himself, dissatisfied with the sums he had appropriated, pondered the mounting balance in Nigel's bank and waited for a suitable opportunity to remove both the money and himself beyond the range of Nancy's interference. There was, he considered, no point in moving out until trouble threatened or Nancy's sexual demands became insupportable; but his intelligence warned him that one or the other condition could not be long delayed. For although he was greedy, he was also wary, knowing that the gods are jealous of prosperity and easily bored by their own favourites.

PART THREE

The Last Match

XII

One morning, entirely by chance, Hugo met Jennifer Stevens. She looked a little tarnished by the London winter but otherwise as appetizing as ever. She accepted an invitation to lunch.

"Why aren't you at Cambridge?" Hugo asked.

"I got bored," said Jennifer. "I don't think they were sorry to see me go. I was beginning to have a reputation."

"So what are you doing?"

"A little modelling. Nothing much. Daddy seems happy to pay my rent and a bit more. I think he hopes I'll marry a marquis. What about you?"

Hugo, thinking she would find it amusing, told her. He was right. Jennifer went into peals of laughter.

"I love that bit about you and Nancy What's-her-name at the party," she said. "What exactly did you do?"

"If you'll invite me back to your flat for a glass of brandy, I'll show you," Hugo said.

Jennifer went red with excitement.

"Get the bill," she said, "get it *now*."

After that, Hugo and Jennifer met quite often, usually in the afternoons, Hugo didn't find it too difficult to fit these meetings in between business appointments, but he did find that they absorbed a lot of the energy which be might otherwise have used for Nancy's benefit. Nancy, aware that Hugo's response to her demands was slackening, began to be resentful and suspicious. Although she made no overt accusations, it was plain from her voice and manner that she thought she was not getting full value. When Hugo confided his uneasiness to Jennifer, she suggested that he should take a course of pills. His reaction to this joke was morose.

"You were always heartless," he said.

"If you can't satisfy us both," Jennifer answered, "you must leave one of us."

That was what Hugo thought. Indeed, his plans for leaving Nancy and Chester Row were now nearly mature. But he was not so sure that he wanted to leave Nancy simply in order to cleave to Jennifer, and in any case he believed very sincerely in travelling alone on occasions of retreat. His departure from Chester Row was certainly going to be that; in fact "retreat" was too dignified a word – the operative term was "flight". Of course, if one had to be accompanied while fleeing, then Jennifer would be as suitable and resourceful a companion as any; but the presence even of Jennifer would violate the elementary rule: "Down to Gehenna or up to the Throne," he quoted to himself. "He travels the fastest who travels alone." (Kipling: he knew a thing or two when it came to practical emergencies.) And then there was that other elementary rule, to which Lionel of all people had introduced him, about keeping your mouth shut. No; he was not going to confide his intentions to Jennifer and risk having everything spoilt at the last minute. For by now it almost was the last minute: his plans would be put into action after a grand chemmy party to celebrate Henry Jarvis' birthday, which would fall in four days' time.

In Santa Kytherea there was increasing nationalist activity, mostly in the form of raids on stores or armouries; but Nigel Palairet's battalion in Port Orestes was left in peace.

"This is too boring," they all said, "let's have a party."

So a party was arranged. Although it was not the first, it was going to be the biggest and most splendid. There was going to be champagne, dancing in a marquee, and a roulette game organized by Nigel, for like all the better regiments the Eleventh Battalion of the Carbinier Guards had found time to train a cadre of corporals as croupiers. All the local English officials and their wives were invited, and several officers asked their Santa Kytherean mistresses, despite the protests of the colonel, who was a regular soldier and knew what was what. The whole battalion was kept busy for days doing the necessary fatigues, the men were quite grateful to have something to do at last, particularly as they were paid a lot of extra money out of the Mess funds, but there were several trouble-makers who, though not slow to draw the extra money, went about saying that it was all wrong and that they weren't in Santa Kytherea just for the officers to amuse themselves. Some such feeling had been anticipated, and in order to put a stop to any grumbling it was arranged that there should be free beer in the men's canteen on the night of the party. The agitators described this as a sop to the masses, but most of the men liked the idea too much to pay any attention to them, for the time being at any rate. In case things should get right out of control, Willie Culbertson arranged that a company under a reliable sergeant-major should be detailed off to remain sober; this would perform the routine security duties and would get its own turn at the free beer on the following night. All in all, it was felt that things had been very equitably arranged.

The officers' party began with éclat. There were two sergeants in full dress to examine the invitation cards, a highly coloured cold buffet, enough champagne to float Buckingham Palace and all the sycophants inside it, and a special bar with brandy and whisky for the soaks. Nigel's roulette table was very popular (although some of the officials' wives seemed to regard it as a hospitable device for distributing money and were very angry when they were asked to pay their losses). But what might have been a thoroughly pleasant and extravagant occasion was to become memorable for the least desirable of reasons.

The rank and file, drinking their free beer in the canteen, became at first jolly, then uproarious, then vicious. The trouble-makers, appreciating the possibilities of this condition, went from group to group and pointed out that they had all been fobbed off with a few pints of beer in return for which they had slaved for days to gratify their officers' love of entertainment and splendour. This might be just tolerable, the agitators conceded, if they were on Regular Army engagements. But they weren't; they were family men, thousands of miles from home, being poorly paid for rotting on an island where they had nothing to do except cater for the whims of a few aristocrats. Mention of their families stirred the men's memories and then their passions. Someone used the word "rights": in thirty seconds the word was on every tongue: somebody, somehow, was conspiring to deny them their *rights*. There was only one quarter where redress could be sought: from their officers. The officers must give them their rights, or else…

Some of the quieter and more level-headed men slipped away while this was going on, but the ringleaders had no difficulty in mustering a hundred malcontents to march on the officers' compound. "We want our rights," the chant went up, "we want our rights."

The colonel, who was benevolently watching Nigel's roulette game and had remained, since he was the chief host, entirely sober, was one of the few people to hear the approaching mob. He waited politely until Nigel had paid out on the last *coup* and then tapped him on the shoulder.

"Five minutes' interval, dear boy," he said, "fetch Willie and join me outside."

Thus it was that when the marchers came to a halt outside the marquee they were met by the colonel and Willie Culbertson, both of whom were regular soldiers and so wore scarlet Mess Dress, and by Nigel, who was wearing a very expensive dinner-jacket. Confronted by symbols both of military tyranny and of upper-class civilian luxury, the crowd broke into an angry boo. The colonel held up a hand for silence and the boo, rather surprisingly, subsided.

"What do you want?" said the colonel equably.

A chant of "We want our rights" was started by one of the ringleaders but was so palpably ridiculous in the face of the colonel's affability that it died immediately.

"If you have any legitimate complaint, choose your spokesmen and send them to me in the morning," the colonel said.

It was no part of the agitators' scheme of things that the occasion should be dominated by rational good sense of this nature. An incident was needed, such an incident as would involve the disgrace of the battalion and its departure from the island, such an incident as could only be whipped up by an appeal to passion or by the sight of blood.

"Bloody Fascist," shouted one of the chief troublemakers, secure in the dark and the crowd. A large stone flew past the colonel's head and landed harmlessly against the wall of the marquee. "Bloody Fascist," the shout went up, and more stones, thrown with a recklessness inspired by beer and a corresponding inaccuracy, shot past the colonel and his aides. Alarmed for the old gentleman's safety, Nigel stepped in front of him and promptly took the only well directed shot of the evening full in the face. When he fell to the ground, the crowd, most of which had only been playing a drunken game, was instantly shamed into silence. Two or three men came forward to see if they could help Nigel. The rest, with the trouble-makers among them, shuffled away into the darkness. Inside the marquee the battalion band, which had played at full strength throughout the incident, broke into *The Vienna Woods*. The guests affected to know nothing of what had occurred but started to leave a few minutes later; the first to do so might have seen Nigel Palairet being put into an ambulance on a stretcher.

"Your boyfriend's coming home," said Jennifer to Hugo.

"My boyfriend?"

"Nancy Palairet's husband, Nigel. It's all in the paper." Hugo took the paper and read a highly-coloured account of a "mutiny" in the Eleventh Battalion of the Carbinier Guards. It also appeared that the day after the party the battalion had at last been involved, willy-nilly, in some minor action; that the authorities were uncertain whether to send it home or not, and were waiting to see how it conducted itself now that it was actually engaged; and that Nigel was in a military hospital suffering from concussion and some unspecified trouble in one eye.

"It doesn't say anything about him coming home," Hugo said.

"No. But he obviously will if he's been badly hurt. So now you'd better be good and quick about whatever you're planning to do."

"How do you know I'm planning to do anything?"

"Just a guess. You are, aren't you?"

"It's none of your business," Hugo said.

"Oh but it is. You needn't think you're going to get clean away with the loot and leave little Jennifer out in the cold."

"Who said anything about loot?"

"I know you, Hugo. In many ways we're very alike. I only have to ask myself what I'd do in your place. So you'd better tell me just what's going to happen, dearie, or I might find myself in Chester Row ringing on the doorbell and tipping off Nancy to watch her money box."

Well, Hugo thought, it would be quite nice to confide in somebody. It seemed unavoidable, and at least Jennifer would be an appreciative audience.

"It'll all happen tomorrow night," he began. "Someone called Henry Jarvis – I've told you about him – is giving a party…"

When Hugo had finished, Jennifer giggled rather a lot and said, "You rat. You slimy, stinking rat. And where do I come in?"

"You didn't, until now."

"But what on earth are you going to do with all that money?"

"I am going to lead a leisured and cultivated life," Hugo said, "and devote much of my time to studying the problems of the human situation. I'm going to become an amateur philosopher, you might say."

"And where are you going to do that?"

"I shall keep out of the way for a bit. Not that Nancy can do anything – imagine explaining the whole set-up to the police – but I feel like a holiday and Nigel might turn nasty when he gets home."

"You don't say… And later on?"

"I rather think I shall spend the summers in England," said Hugo complacently, "and the winters abroad. I like cricket, you see, and it's not a good thing to cut oneself off completely from one's own country."

"You haven't got a country," said Jennifer admiringly. "But you still haven't told me what I want to know. Where do I come in? I quite see you were planning to take off without me, but now you'll have to think again, won't you?"

"Very well. Where do you want to come in?"

"I could do with a bit of a holiday myself. I'd like to come away with you when you go and later on, when we get sick of one another again, I'd like a third of the money."

"A *third*? You greedy little bitch."

"It's no good using that sort of language."

"But look here, Jennifer," said Hugo, "I've told you all this in friendly confidence. I really think you're behaving rather badly."

"Hark who's talking. You wouldn't have told me a single bloody thing if I hadn't guessed. Not that that was very hard… A third of the money, Hugo, or else…"

"Or else what?"

"I shall go to the proper authorities and tell them just where it all came from."

"You have a point, my angel. But first things first. If you are coming away with me, you will be needing an air ticket and a vaccination certificate. And then there is the matter of place and time, as poor Nigel Palairet would say. So now, dear, listen to me carefully…"

Now that he no longer had the strain of running the school, James Escome was drinking far less; and although at times he felt lonely and disappointed, in a quiet way be was rather enjoying life. He played golf; he took Georgy and Bessie on a trip to Paris and on down to Aix-en-Provence; and above all he looked forward to the summer, when for the first time in many years he would be free to watch the Kent County Cricket XI play in every single match. Or nearly every match. For James had another reason for looking forward to the summer: he had a project. The Council had now paid for the field but he had been told that no building would start until some time in June. He had asked for and obtained permission to use it until the end of May (Mrs Hunt, to do her justice, was generous in victory), and it was his intention to hold a cricket week – a last, beautiful week of cricket before his field disappeared for ever. He was already beginning to arrange it. He was going to invite some twenty or thirty old friends and favoured old boys of Baron's Lodge and entertain them royally in the school; and every day from May 15th to May 25th they would field an XI against some reputable club side. Since James was known and loved in the cricket world, it was not proving difficult for him to find opponents. One thing the old boy could do, they all said, was to get together a decent side to play them, and he'd certainly see that the food and drink were up to par; besides, he'd had a wretched year and it was up to them to see that his little treat went off well. So James had already been able to arrange fixtures against – among others – Tonbridge School, the Kent County Colts, the Butterflies, the Free Foresters (two days) and the I Zingari; and it was even possible that the MCC itself would send down a side to provide the grand finale.

Only one thing worried James: would Hugo come? For without Hugo it would not be quite the same. If Hugo came, it would be a sign that any awkwardness between them, any sense of blame or guilt, was at an end. Not that James had ever blamed Hugo, but he was afraid Hugo might think he had and he was particularly anxious that any such impression might be laid to rest for good. Besides, he wanted just to *see* Hugo; and then Hugo was a useful player, might well get some runs; and Hugo – Well, leave it be. It was simply that this would be the last occasion of note at Baron's Lodge and he hoped, he prayed, that Hugo would be there.

Anyway, there was Hugo's invitation among the others. Forty invitations in all. He had already spoken to about twenty of those whom he was now inviting and fifteen of them, he gathered, were almost certain to accept. Say there were ten more acceptances from the other twenty he was asking, and that would be fine. Or say they all accepted – splendid, the more the merrier, there was (God knew) plenty of room. So long as Hugo accepted... Happily and hopefully, the old man pottered off to put his invitations in the post.

The morning after his conversation with Jennifer, the same morning that James Escome posted the invitations to his cricket week, Hugo went to his bank and drew out £1,000 in five pound notes. That should be enough, he thought, until... well until, as Jennifer herself had put it, they got tired of one another again.

Then he went back to Chester Row, where to Nancy's delight he spent the entire afternoon making love to her.

Then he had a bath, put on his dinner jacket, and went out to dine alone in the Savoy Grill. He ate fresh Pâté de Foie Gras, Pressed Duck and a green salad with a French dressing; with this meal he drank half a bottle of very fine claret, and he allowed himself a large glass of Armagnac with his coffee.

Then he went to Henry Jarvis' birthday party, where he conducted a game of chemin-de-fer in the normal fashion. The game finished at half past three in the morning, when he wrote out cheques against Nigel's account to the value of about forty-five thousand pounds and received cheques totalling some fifty-one thousand pounds from the losers.

Then he went to the lavatory in order to do some quick sums in private. The firm's account now stood about fifty-three thousand pounds in credit, so that when the cheques which he had just drawn against it had been met it would still be worth eight thousand pounds – rather more than the amount which Nigel had originally put into it and enough to enable Nigel and Nancy to continue comfortably in business with an unblemished reputation. As for the cheques which he had received that evening and which were, as usual, payable to Cash, these he put into an envelope addressed to his own private bank together with a note instructing the manager to have them cleared immediately and credited to his account. All the drawers had become well known to him over the preceding weeks and he had no doubt whatever that the cheques would be honoured. Since he had already salted away nearly ten thousand pounds, he would now have a personal fortune of sixty thousand.

Having made these calculations, he emerged from the lavatory, said good night to Henry Jarvis, and drove back to London. After he had stopped at his bank to push the envelope through the letter-box, he drove on to Jennifer's flat, where he took five minutes to change into an ordinary suit and explain to Jennifer that everything had gone according to plan. His bank manager, he reminded her, would set about clearing the cheques for his credit early the following morning, and since most of them were drawn on London accounts this would not take long. By the time Nancy had missed him (they did not usually get up in Chester Row till half past ten or even, on the morning after chemmy parties, eleven), had become suspicious, found out who had paid him money that night (if it occurred to her to do so), and warned them of her suspicions so that they might cancel their cheques, it would be too late. On hearing all this, Jennifer congratulated him with an ironical kiss on the cheek and carefully checked through her luggage and her documents.

Then they drove to London Airport. They arrived there just before seven a.m., in good time to board the aeroplane on which they had booked their passages to Beirut.

XII

About ten days after Hugo and Jennifer left for Beirut, Nigel Palairet was flown back by the Army from Santa Kytherea. He arrived in Chester Row with a black patch over one eye.

"It's nothing to worry about," he told Nancy, "but they said I could come home if I wanted to and I'd certainly had enough of Santa Kytherea."

"I wonder you went in the first place."

"It seemed the decent thing to do. There were all one's friends, taking it for granted that one would go with them... There was really no choice."

"Then why did you come back?"

"I thought I'd done enough. I went there because it was somehow expected of me. And I stood in front of poor old Colonel Guy when they started throwing stones because one can't let old men get hurt. All, you see, according to the rules. And so then, when the rules said that I myself had been hurt just badly enough to come home, I didn't see why I shouldn't take advantage of them. Besides, I was worried."

"Worried, Nigel?"

"Yes. There was something odd about Hugo when I left. And this business of Baron's Lodge closing down. You'd better tell me what's been happening, Nancy."

"I'm afraid I've made fools of us both."

"You slept with Hugo?"

"Yes."

"I thought you might," Nigel said slowly, "but I don't think it matters, do you?"

"No. Though I'm grateful to you for being so sensible… But I'm afraid that's not all. Hugo's gone, Nigel. And taken a lot of our money."

Nigel hung his head and said nothing.

"It was my fault. I let him sign cheques, let him control the money for the chemmy games. I should have known."

"It was my suggestion that he should do," said Nigel without looking up.

"I know. But I wasn't going to let him because I felt there was something wrong. And then…because I was afraid he might leave me, might stop coming to me, I let him have his way. All the time I knew there was something wrong, Nigel, but I couldn't bear to go without the things he did to me, so I gave in."

"I see," Nigel looked up and smiled at her. "And anyhow, we're both to blame. For trusting him in the first place. What exactly happened? Facts, Nancy, it's too late for regret."

Nancy told him.

"So at least," said Nigel at last, "he's left us some of our money and all of our good name. We'll just have to start again."

"There's no way of getting the money back?"

"No legal way. How could there be? That's why loyalty was always so important. And now tell me what you know about Baron's Lodge."

"They needed money. There was a girl here, James Escome's daughter, who said Hugo had taken money from them which he had no right to. They needed his help as well, I think. The old man couldn't carry on without him."

"At least you could have given them the money."

"Hugo wouldn't let me. And once again I was afraid that if I crossed him… I even justified him to myself."

"Do you know what happened to them all in the end?" Nigel asked.

"No," said Nancy. "The subject wasn't mentioned again. It made Hugo angry, so I didn't like to ask. I didn't really want to know."

Nigel nodded dismissively.

"Well," he said, "there's three things to be done. Hugo is to be forgotten. We must start making money again. And we must offer to help James Escome, if it's not too late. We owe him that. I'll go and see him as soon as we've straightened things out here…"

Hugo and Jennifer hired a car and drove from Beirut to Baalbek.

"The last time I came here," he said, "it was with Nigel and Nancy Palairet."

"Why mention them?" said Jennifer crossly.

"I feel regretful about them," said Hugo. He looked up at the towering Roman columns. "I was fond of them, you see."

"So fond of them that you cheated them of a fortune."

"You can exploit people without ceasing to like them. You're in the process of blackmailing me, but you seem to enjoy my company."

"I shan't enjoy it much longer," Jennifer said, "if you keep making me come to look at ruins. They're so morbid. They make me feel that I'm dead."

"There are some of the finest Roman remains in the Near East."

"They still make me feel that I'm dead."

"Well, what do you like doing?" Hugo said patiently.

"I like having attention," Jennifer said.

"You were always honest about your own character… Will it do any good if I explain to you what these ruins are all about?"

"Not a bit of good. I should like to get back to the hotel in Beirut in time for dinner. After that we can go to the Casino. I want to get away from these beastly pillars. Now."

"Very well." They began to walk down a massive flight of steps. "But why," said Hugo, "did you let me bring you here in the first place?"

"For the drive. I like being on the move. Let's leave Beirut tomorrow and go somewhere else."

"Certainly. We can easily get a plane to Cyprus. Or Istanbul. Athens. Anywhere."

"I've always wanted," Jennifer said, "to go to Jerusalem."

"*Jerusalem?*"

"Yes. You've met Daddy. Didn't you notice? He's half Jewish. He doesn't go to a synagogue or anything, and sometimes I think he's rather ashamed of it. But I'm not. They say a little Jewish blood adds a lot of spice."

"In your case, daughter of Jerusalem, they are quite right. But we can't go direct from the Lebanon. Tomorrow," said Hugo, who was amused and slightly touched, "we'd better fly to Cyprus, where we shall be able to get a visa. From Nicosia to Tel-Aviv should not be difficult, and in Tel-Aviv we can hire another car…"

"Well, well," said James Escome, "Nigel Palairet. It's very good to see you, Nigel, after all this time. Just passing through?"

"No, sir. I came especially to see you."

"That was nice, Nigel. And how's Hugo? You and he have got some enterprise going, I hear. I'd been hoping to see something – "

He checked himself and lowered his eyes.

"It's because of Hugo that I came, sir."

"Is there anything wrong with him?" said James rather wildly. "He's all right, isn't he? Come on, boy, tell me."

"As far as I know, he's quite all right," Nigel said, "he's away at the moment."

"Ah," said James happily, "that's why he hasn't answered the invitation."

"Invitation, sir?"

"I'll tell you about that later. I didn't send you one because Georgy said you were in Santa Kytherea."

"What else did she say?"

"Just that she'd happened to meet your lady wife, that Hugo was living and working with you both, but that you were away with the Carbiniers."

"Nothing more than that?"

"What more would there be? Though I'd have liked to know what you were all up to."

"We're agents," said Nigel.

"Agents for what?"

"Almost anything."

"Very handy," said James dubiously. And then, "I suppose you'd better tell me what you came about."

"It's rather difficult…" Nigel paused and thought of Georgiana. A sensible, helpful girl, he remembered. And now it appeared that she had kept from her father the real circumstances and motives of her visit to Chester Row. It also appeared that James, so far from resenting Hugo's desertion, was only anxious to hear about his welfare. It appeared, in fact, that James had only the haziest idea of what was going on and that Georgiana, no doubt in her father's own interest, had not seen fit to enlighten him. If Georgiana thought it best to encourage her father in his illusions about Hugo, it was hardly for him, Nigel, to interfere.

"Come on, boy," said James rather sharply. "You said it had something to do with Hugo, I think?"

"Only indirectly," Nigel said. "You see, sir, both Hugo and I have been very busy, and we've been away a lot, so of course we didn't really know what was going on down here. But now it seems – well, it seems you've had trouble."

"Things have been difficult since Lionel's death," said James with dignity, "as indeed they were bound to be."

"Hugo was worried about that," Nigel found himself saying, "but he seemed to think you could get by. Now that you've actually closed, the truth has been brought home to both of us. What I thought was...and I know if Hugo were here he'd be with me in this...what I'm trying to say is, is there anything I can do that will be of help now?" He drew a deep breath. "Do you need money, sir?" he said. "If so, there is money available."

James turned down his eyes for a moment, then looked up at Nigel and smiled.

"It's very good of you to worry about me," he said, "very good." Then he looked puzzled. "But didn't Hugo tell you?" he went on. "I certainly wrote to him about it. Since we shan't need the field any more I've arranged to sell it. On very good terms. Didn't he tell you about that?"

"He hasn't really had a chance," said Nigel with a straight face. "He left before I got back from Santa Kytherea."

"But you might have known," said James gently, "that if we had needed help badly, Hugo would have seen to it before he left. So there was really no need for you to come, was there?"

For a moment Nigel wanted to take James by the shoulder and shake the truth into him, to tell him that Hugo wouldn't move a finger to save him from an eternity in hell, let alone from present ruin. But then he saw the love in the old man's eyes, and he reflected that Georgiana, upright and honourable as he always remembered her, had not scrupled to tell lies in order that James might keep this love, and he told himself, part bitterly and part ironically, that pity must come before truth.

"I didn't really think," he muttered. "I suddenly heard you'd closed, so I just came down..."

"And I'm glad you came," said James. "Come along now. We'll go for a little walk on the field while we still can."

"Where's the pavilion?" said Nigel, as they walked across the field towards the square at its centre.

"They took it away."

"It seems so sad that there will be no more cricket."

"Ah, but there will. That's what I meant when I was talking of those invitations." He told Nigel of his plans for May. "One last week – ten days really, but one always calls it a week – one last week of cricket before the field goes for good. You'll come, Nigel, won't you? Now that you're home again, you'll come?"

"I wouldn't miss it for the world," Nigel said.

"I know tennis and rackets were always more your thing," James burbled on, "but you were in the twenty-two at Eton, and anyway you're a friend of Hugo's. And that's another thing. Will Hugo be back in time? And where can we get hold of him?"

"I'm not quite sure –" Nigel began.

" – You see," said James, who had hardly heard him, "it will make all the difference if Hugo can come. It's going to be our last little flutter, and apart from Georgy, Hugo's the only one left in the family. He ought to be here, Nigel, and of course we all want to see him so much –"

He caught himself up.

"But I'm being a bore," he said, "excuse me."

"I know what you mean, sir," Nigel said. "Will you leave it to me? I'll make sure he knows."

"Don't you trouble yourself, my dear boy. Just give me his address and I'll write."

"I'm afraid it's rather complicated," said Nigel as naturally as he could. "You see, sir, Hugo is moving from place to place…anywhere he hears there might be something in our line at a moment's notice. But he gets in touch with me every few days to tell me how things are going. So if you leave it all to me, I'll make sure… I'll make sure he comes, sir, I promise you that."

"Well, it's very kind of you," said James. "And I expect you're right. That way we shall be certain. Would you like to have a quick look at the tennis courts? I always remember those games you and Lionel used to have…"

"I shall have to find Hugo," Nigel said to Nancy that night. "If necessary, I must go myself and look for him."

"But Nigel... With all the work we've got. So much ground to make up."

"I know. But if you'd seen that old man today, you'd understand. It's the least I can do, Nancy. After all, it was my fault Hugo didn't go back to Baron's Lodge when he was needed."

"You weren't to know, my dear," Nancy said. "You tried to make sure before you took Hugo on."

"I didn't try hard enough; I just accepted what Hugo told me. The least I can do is bring Hugo to the old man now."

"But it's only for a few days of cricket," Nancy persisted, "surely – "

" – No," said Nigel. "It's no good arguing, Nancy. I must and will find Hugo Warren and *make* him go to Baron's Lodge in May."

XIII

In Jerusalem Hugo and Jennifer stayed at the King David Hotel. "What a sexy place Jerusalem is," Jennifer (predictably) remarked.

"I can't say I'd noticed it. Tel-Aviv, yes. Sea air and all those pretty children. But Jerusalem."

"The children are just as pretty here."

"It puts me off," Hugo said, "to think of all those orthodox Jews. Ringlets and woollen stockings. Ugh."

"You're being anti-Semitic."

"Rubbish. Just anti-Jewish-orthodox. Which is what most of the Jews themselves are."

"Well, sexy or not," said Jennifer, "I don't think I shall want to stay here long. But there's one place I'd like to see before we leave."

"Oh?"

"Sodom." She giggled and thrust her naked rump at him.

"But these days, my dear" – he patted her behind patronizingly – "Sodom is just a collection of huts on the edge of the Dead Sea. A Post Office, a hostel for student hikers... All the *activities* stopped several millennia ago."

"What about the student hikers?"

"Israeli students are much too serious for that kind of thing."

"Nevertheless," said Jennifer, "I want to go to Sodom. I like the name so much. The leaflet says there's a restaurant. And you can bathe, it says. The Dead Sea's so salt that you can't sink."

"Indeed? And how does one get there?"

"We can drive. The road goes right through the desert. It says here it'll take about an hour and a half from Jerusalem."

"Very well. Tomorrow?"

"Tomorrow."

When Hugo was back in his room, he considered the problem of Jennifer. Up till now she had been, on the whole, good company, and although they made love less than they used to he still found her sexually exhilarating. But very soon now they would tire of one another; in any case there was a limit to the time and money he wished to spend on someone so fundamentally sterile. When the day came for them to part, she was going to demand upwards of fifteen thousand pounds (and what was to prevent her coming back for more later?) as the price of her silence; nor did he have any doubt that she was fully capable, if refused the money, of going to the police and telling them what kind of organization was working in Chester Row. Now, what would happen then? As he saw it, Nigel, Nancy and himself would be liable to charges of living off immoral earnings, or something very similar; they would all qualify, if he was to believe his newspapers, for very nasty sentences indeed. No doubt he, Hugo, could stay abroad for a time, thus avoiding arrest; but even if he wanted to – which he didn't – he could not stay abroad forever. The passport people would see to that. It followed that Jennifer's sanction was ultimately valid. What was to be done?

If only he had never told her about Nigel and Nancy: it was intolerable that a few words, spoken in a state of mildly drunken infatuation at luncheon in a London restaurant, should be costing him so dear. If only he had never met Jennifer at all (damn Harold and his springtime parties). But it was no good going into all that. The facts were what they were, they must be faced and dealt with. And the sooner the better. All this fiddling about in the Levant was getting on his nerves and bringing him no nearer to the good life – that mixture of sensual and intellectual pursuits – which he had promised himself as the reward of his astuteness and, more important, as the justification of his treachery. No one could lead the good life with Jennifer around.

He stood by his window and looked out at the two little hills which rival traditions call Calvary. Mounds, he thought, mounds of dust; rubbish dumps. What was that absurd hymn? "There is a green hill far away…" A typical falsity. He thought with pleasure of the party of pious Americans he had observed that morning. They had come in a bus on a day trip from Tel-Aviv: "Tour of Holy Places. $10 with two meals (non-Kosher)." Their guide had brought them to some vantage point where Jennifer and he were loitering, had pointed out the two Calvaries and had started to explain the opposing theories. "But say," an indignant woman had whined, "*neither* of them's big enough." A popular fallacy – that the Romans knew the importance of the occasion and should have chosen a venue to accord with it. "But, madam," the Israeli guide had said rather acidly, "you don't need a mountain for a routine execution."

And now, in his room, Hugo pondered this proposition again. You certainly didn't need a mountain; a desert would do just as well. Let's see now… "Come on, Jennifer, I'm feeling sexy. Let's get out and have some dick." "Here in the desert, Hugo?" "Why not? A fine and private place, like the grave, Jennifer." "Ooh, I do love it when you're morbid, Hugo. Like that time just after your cousin died. Do you remember? Let's do it like that. I can hardly wait." Slamming of car doors. "Down here, Jennifer, in this gully. No one will come. No one will see." "Ooooh…" Then, a little later. "You're hurting, Hugo…Hugo, stop it…Hugoooo…" Car doors slam again and engine starts into life. Turn back a few minutes later, and what do you see? Vultures wheeling over the desert (vultures are *very* quick at picking up bad news); vultures wheeling…vultures swooping… Drive on fast. Question: How long before the vultures picked her clean? Answer: A few hours; three, perhaps less. And your authority for this statement, Mr Warren? Lawrence whom he had taught at Baron's Lodge the previous spring. Lawrence had been born in India, knew all about vultures (they had caught his imagination), and had produced some pithily turned facts about them in the course of a five minute lecturette to the rest of the Common Entrance Candidates. Even if allowance were made for a juvenile tendency to exaggerate, surely the body would be *unrecognizable* within three hours; and tradition said that if you did not have an identifiable corpse, you did not have a murder. Which might be unfair to some, but was only, if you thought about it, logical.

Now then. Place and time (as Nigel might have said) and administration. You booked out of the King David Hotel in the morning, before leaving for Sodom. ("Pack your kit up, dear. We'll find somewhere amusing to spend the night... Ascalon, I thought. You know, tell it not in the streets...and they say the wines there are very good.") You drove to Sodom, bathed, had lunch, drove back across the empty desert, perhaps turned down a side-track if there was one. "Come on, Jennifer, I'm feeling sexy..." Etc., etc.... Then you drove straight to Tel-Aviv, which would take about three hours to judge from the map, so that you reached Tel-Aviv quite early in the evening. You left Jennifer's luggage, with her passport, etc., packed inside it, at a left luggage office, drove to the car hire people, collected your deposit, took a taxi to the airport, took a plane wherever a plane with an empty seat was going. By which time, Jennifer Stevens was a pile of anonymous bones under the cold stars.

Important point: *no* clothes or other means of identification must be left on her. The vultures must have their feast strictly *nature*. Possible objection: suppose someone came along and interrupted the darling birds? Answer: people don't loiter about in a desert; anyone there is only passing through, passing through as quickly as possible, and an instinct stronger than mere curiosity tells a man to give a wide berth to vultures at work. There would probably be no one to see the birds; if there were, he would not disturb them; if he did, it would probably be too late; and even if it weren't, he himself would be off to a flying (literally) start.

Why am I so cool about this? Hugo thought. Why can I think of murdering Jennifer, at the same moment as I think of coupling with her, without a single qualm of remorse or regret. But of course Jennifer is not really a human being at all; she's just a function – a function of cells, glands, tissues, etc., which one can terminate with as little worry as one would turn off a machine. Well, that was it; turn off the coupling machine which was Jennifer Stevens and save yourself fifteen thousand pounds. And then, perhaps, the good life could begin.

"The younger men and the bachelors," said James to Georgy, "can sleep in the boys' dormitories. Elder married men can have the junior masters' rooms."

Although there were some weeks to go, they were discussing the arrangements for the cricket week.

"But surely," said Georgy, "they'll none of them bring their wives."

"Not if I can help it. But there comes a time of life when one expects privacy."

"Well, we've got five small rooms that the assistant masters used to have and two bigger ones – Lionel's and Hugo's. Which makes seven."

"Hugo will want his own room," said James.

"But, Daddy, are you sure?"

"Yes. So that means the six senior married men can have rooms to themselves. The rest get the barrack room treatment. So far we've got twenty-six people coming, which means at least three dormitories will be wanted. All right?" he said crisply.

"All right, Daddy," said Georgians.

Later on, Georgiana said to Bessie, "I'm glad about this cricket week because Daddy's so happy making the arrangements. But I do wish he wasn't so certain about Hugo. It'll break his heart if he doesn't come."

"No use worrying, love," Bessie said. "Nigel Palairet's said he'll get him here, and he was always a boy to stick by his word."

"But you know how…elusive… Hugo can be."

"Then good riddance, if you ask me."

"But what will Daddy do?"

"Your father will have to face the facts sometime."

"I think it might finally kill him," Georgiana said.

"Now," said Hugo to Jennifer, "pack up all your stuff and be ready to leave at half past ten."

"But – ?"

" – We'll find somewhere else to spend the night. You said you were sick of Jerusalem."

They drove through mean, scrubby hills which later flattened off into crude grazing land, dotted here and there with Arab tents. Then, almost unnoticed, the scrub had become desert.

"They call this the Negev," Hugo said. "They are cultivating parts of it, very successfully it seems. But there is a lot left over."

They drove east towards the mountains of Moab. "We are on the border between the wilderness and the promised land," Hugo said. "To the south you see what Moses had to contend with. Not to mention the personal difficulties."

"How odd you're being," said Jennifer.

"I'm in an odd mood. I find this desert unsettling."

The road was modern and in good condition, but on either side the desert rolled away, rock and sand. Every now and then, Hugo noticed, there were rough tracks leading off the main road. Then they began to descend. Above the road towered walls of rock which glistened in the sun.

"Salt," said Hugo, when Jennifer inquired about this. "You remember what happened to Lot's wife?"

159

"It always seemed rather unfair. I mean, she was only looking back to say goodbye."

"Her mistake," said Hugo, "was to look back with regret. Nothing is more paralysing than regret."

They rounded a corner and there, sluggish and inhospitable, lay the Dead Sea.

"Will there be Dead Sea fruit?" asked Jennifer.

"No. It's only an image. Like Lot's wife... And here is the city of Sodom."

They drove past a few huts and stopped by a neatly appointed restaurant.

"You see?" said Jennifer. "A lovely restaurant. I told you."

The manager of the restaurant let them have a room in which to change before they bathed in the Dead Sea. The floor of the sea was of a curious brittle substance. If you did not tread carefully, your feet went through and into the slime below. This happened to both of them several times; each time their legs went through, they were badly cut.

After bathing, they had to have a shower to get the salt off. The blood on their calves excited them so much that they made love in the shower, standing up. After this they had lunch and a brisk bottle of red wine from Ascalon.

Well, thought Hugo, as they drove back uphill and past the pillars of salt, it's been a nice day out. It's been nice knowing you. It's such a pity...if only you weren't so greedy. I'll give you one more chance to make sure.

"Jennifer," he said, "when we get back to England I'll give you five thousand pounds. How's that?"

"Very nice, as far as it goes. The only trouble is that we agreed on more. One third of what you took."

"You don't know what I took. I never told you and you never asked."

"I didn't need to. You always said that on those chemmy evenings you used to pay out anything up to eighty thousand

and take in as much as ninety or a hundred. Say this time was an average evening – say the losers paid you about sixty thousand. That makes twenty thousand for Jennifer. I think that's fair, don't you? Twenty thousand."

"I'll give you ten thousand," he said. "Five when we get home and five in a year's time."

"You'll give me twenty thousand," she said, "and you'll give it me all at once."

"As you know," said Hugo, "I'm in no position to argue. Don't let's quarrel about it. We were having such fun."

"Who's quarrelling?" Jennifer said.

After a little while, Hugo turned up a track which led through a small ravine.

"Where are we going?" Jennifer asked.

"Not far. Just to get the feel of the desert."

They emerged from the ravine into a rough amphitheatre of rock. Hugo stopped the car.

"Christ," Jennifer said, "I'm feeling randy again already. It must be the desert. Let's get out."

"I was just going to suggest the same thing myself. But do you think the desert is suitable?"

"No one about that I can see. Hurry up, Hugo, I can hardly wait. Let's pretend we're Nancy and you at that party. I almost wish there was someone to see us."

"I don't," said Hugo, slowly caressing her throat.

"Oh, oh," she said after a minute or two, "I don't think it's ever been so good as this."

"I'm glad. Make the most of it."

"Oh, oh," she said, "Hugo, Hugo, oh, Hugo, it's so good that I could die with it."

"I'm afraid you're going to," he said, tightening his grip around her throat.

Fifteen minutes later, when Hugo looked back down the main road, the vultures were already wheeling down over the little ravine. He let the clutch in and started to drive fast but carefully towards the coast.

Nigel Palairet was a man of his word. He had promised to find Hugo, and although this would be tiresome he had a persistent nature and many connections to help him. By courtesy of officials at London Airport he was able to check the flight lists for the day Hugo had vanished; and a few days later, when he had put his affairs in good trim, he left Nancy in charge and flew to Beirut. Here a few inquiries in likely hotels revealed that Hugo, accompanied by a woman called Miss Jennifer Stevens, had stayed a few nights and left on such a date; the flight lists for the appropriate date instructed him where to proceed next, a few more inquiries in hotels directed him to further flight lists, and at length, after some days of dispensing bribes to clerks and receptionists and hunting through mounds of paper, he found himself in Venice. First he tried the Gritti Palace, then the Danieli, then the Luna. Third time lucky. Yes, Mr Hugo Warren was staying in the hotel, but was out at the moment. No, they had no Miss Stevens. Nigel, who had not expected that they would have a Miss Stevens and had been curious about her ever since finding that she had not left Israel on the same plane as Hugo, sat down in the hall to wait.

When, two hours later, Hugo stepped out of a motor-boat on to the hotel quay and came in through the massive glass door, Nigel rose, smiled, waved to him, went to him, put his arm round his shoulder, and led him to the bar.

"There is nothing to worry about," Nigel said, "but I have something important to say to you. Your uncle is holding a cricket week in May and he very much wants you to be there."

"You came all the way here to tell me *that*?"

"It is, as I say, important." Nigel then explained why. "Because of my respect for your uncle," he went on, "I shall behave to you there as though nothing had happened. The only way such behaviour can be made convincing is for me really to believe nothing has happened. You can keep the money and I shall forget the whole thing."

There was a long pause. Then, "Why," inquired Hugo, "are you prepared to go to such lengths simply on account of Uncle James?"

"If you don't understand now," said Nigel evenly, "you never will. You must take it that I am prepared on condition you come to Baron's Lodge in May, to accept you, and indeed really to think of you, as my friend."

"But cannot *you* understand," said Hugo, "why it is impossible for me to go there? Why it was always impossible?"

"Tell me why."

"Because they all stifle me. They put a false belief in me, Nigel, they erected a pretence around me, they put me in a glass case marked 'Precious Object'. To judge from what you say, Uncle James still sees me in this case."

"And will it do you any harm to exhibit yourself to him?"

"I've told you. The position was intolerable. If I couldn't go back there last autumn, how do you imagine I can do so now?"

"But, Hugo, it's only for a few days. It'll give so much pleasure and you needn't even stay the entire week. Just play in one or two matches, then I'll tell the old boy we've got important business."

"All I want to do is forget him. And be forgotten. Why won't he just leave me alone?"

"Because he loves you."

"How many times do I have to tell you?" snarled Hugo. "I don't want his love. It's the one reproach which I can't bear. Anything else, hatred, scorn, derision, disgrace, all these I can endure or despise, but not Uncle James' love."

"Then you won't come?"

"Look, Hugo." It was only an outside shot, Nigel told himself, little more than a gambit to keep the conversation going, but it might just lead somewhere. "What happened to Jennifer Stevens?"

For the hundredth part of a second there was fear in Hugo's eyes. Then it was gone. It told Nigel nothing specific; only that there was a weakness here which he might be able to exploit.

"What do you know of Jennifer?" said Hugo peevishly. "What concern is she of yours?"

"I only know that she was with you and that now she isn't. I just wondered."

"We separated. We'd had enough of one another, that's all."

"And where is she now?"

"Still in Israel, I suppose. She was partly Jewish, you see, and wanted to stay on there a bit, I didn't, and that was one of the reasons why we split up."

"I see."

"We quarrelled in Jerusalem," Hugo went on, as if repeating a set lesson, "and we quarrelled again the next day on the way to Sodom. Then we agreed it was no good going on like that, so I drove Jennifer to Tel-Aviv, left her there and caught a plane to Athens."

"You shouldn't press details on people who don't ask for them" said Nigel, who was now a little more sure of his ground. "It might make them suspicious."

"What can you mean?"

"Let me put it this way." Even now, he told himself, even after that odd speech of Hugo's, it was still a thousand to one chance; but it was just worth trying. "Your uncle's cricket week starts in about four weeks' time. I shall be there on the first day – May the fifteenth. If you are not there by May the eighteenth, Hugo, I shall ring up Scotland Yard and tell them that a certain Miss Jennifer Stevens left England with you in March for Beirut, Cyprus and Jerusalem, and has not yet returned. I shall suggest they call on her parents, make an inquiry or two. No doubt, I shall say, everything's in order – "

" – As it is and will be – "

" – But nevertheless, I shall say, her friends are beginning to be concerned. That's all."

"And if I am at Baron's Lodge?"

"Miss Stevens means nothing to me," Nigel said. "I'm only worried about James Escome."

Sooner rather than later, Hugo thought, they'll start looking for Jennifer. Her father will wonder why her letters have stopped, there'll be inquiries, they'll trace her to Israel. They'll find nothing there, so then they'll come to me. I shan't put myself in their way but I shall make no attempt to avoid them; I shall just sit here in Venice leading the good life, and when they do come I shall give them my full co-operation. "This is where we went, that's what we did, I haven't seen her since." They may well come to me even before Uncle James' cricket week. So why worry about what Nigel can do? He can only put them on a trail which some time or another they're bound to find for themselves and which in any case will lead them nowhere at all.

Nigel, who reasoned along much the same lines as Hugo, realized that even if his general hypothesis was correct, even even if something – he did not know quite what, but something rather unpleasant – had indeed happened to Jennifer Stevens, his threat was still not enough to bring Hugo to Baron's Lodge. He needed more evidence. So he went to Israel. He made some discreet and apparently casual inquiries, he drove hither and thither to Jerusalem and Haifa and down to the Dead Sea. Since he reasoned along much the same lines as Hugo, he spent a lot of time on the road to Sodom.

Then, despite expense and difficulty, he rang up the Hotel Luna in Venice. Mr Warren was still there, they said; he had warned them he would be staying indefinitely. Having learnt this, Nigel sat down to write a letter.

May 7

Dear Hugo (he wrote),
Have you ever seen a skeleton? I had thought, from my reading of detective stories, that they kept their teeth; but

165

after vultures have been at their cheeks and gums, their teeth are sadly disarranged. No longer identifiable, I should say, even by the dentist who last worked on them. In any case, I don't suppose Miss Stevens had to have much done to her young and healthy little mouth.

No doubt you took this into account along with *almost* everything else. But one thing you forgot. A neat little device that any prudent and unmarried girl will wear on intimate occasions, and which she has probably procured, after a special fitting, from one of a limited number of clinics – which no doubt keep records and can recognize their own handiwork even though it may be a bit weathered.

I hope I shall be spared the trouble of going round these dreary places; and as you know, I wouldn't dream of making trouble for the sake of moral principle. But I am concerned that James Escome should not be hurt. If you come to Baron's Lodge, he will be happy. If not, he will be so unhappy that it will be much better that you should be exposed, to him and to everyone else, for what you are. There is no point in preserving your uncle's illusions for him unless they are to give him pleasure; if he is to have pain, then he might just as well have the truth along with it.

I look forward to seeing you at Baron's Lodge in May.
Yours ever,

Nigel

XIV

On may the seventeenth Hugo returned to Baron's Lodge. He left his luggage at the station and walked up Church Straight. When he had passed the shopkeepers' villas and the birds began to sing to him from the trees and meadows, he was reminded how they had once sung to him of his love for Jennifer. He thought of Jennifer in the desert ("It's never been so good") and was seized with a fit of lust for her; then he thought of Nigel scrabbling about among the poor, violated bones, and desire died. When he came to the disused graveyard, he hesitated, looked about him to see that no one was watching him, and walked over to Lionel's grave. Since he had last been there, on the day of the funeral, a stone had been placed at its head, unpolished and unornamented save by a legend cut in plain characters:

LIONEL ESCOME, ESQRE.,
OF BARON'S LODGE
1923–95–.

Hic manus ob patriam pugnando volnera passi.

"I'm sorry, Lionel," he said out loud, "I didn't mean to kill you."

He looked guiltily round to see if there had been anyone to hear. Come, come, he thought, this will never do; if Lionel knows anything he certainly knows that. The point is now, what am I to do here? How am I to behave? For the first time since Lionel was buried, I have come, under pressure, to Baron's Lodge. By what means can I make the time pass as painlessly as possible? Bessie will see me as a traitor and treat me with contempt; I can bear that and I can, for the most part, avoid her. Georgy also will see me as a traitor, but she will disguise her feelings so as not to upset Uncle James. And he will see me...see me as what? A prodigal? But he affects not to know that I have strayed; as far as he is concerned I just chose to pursue a career elsewhere and he himself was always very firm that I should not come back to teach here just for family reasons. No; Uncle James will see me as he did a year ago – as his second son coming home for a brief holiday from a legitimate occupation. As to my occupation, he knows nothing, so that's all right; the trouble is that his first son has now died, thus bestowing on the second a role which he does not want and cannot fill. (Not to mention the fact that "the brief holiday" coincides with a somewhat emotional occasion – with the funeral, in a sense, of Baron's Lodge itself.) So how to play it so as to avoid anger or embarrassment? Both of which (for will not Nigel be watching?) must be avoided. But I've got one thing on my side, he told himself: *I just don't care any more.* That's what I must cling to – my indifference. No need to worry about what anyone else does or says; just ignore it. All I need do is play cricket, behave correctly, talk politely, discourage, by a cool demeanour, any tendency to gush or to lament. That's it, boy: play it *cool.* Then perhaps Uncle James will at last get the message and leave me alone for good.

"Hugo...Hugo, my dear boy."

And there was his uncle standing beside him.

"I just slipped away from the cricket for a moment. I like to come here sometimes, you see. I'm glad that you too – But how are you, Hugo?"

"Well, Uncle James. And you?"

"Mustn't complain. It's been a bad year, as you've heard. But things are better now – more settled. And we've got all this cricket to look forward to. It's the County Colts today, the Butterflies tomorrow. And the MCC is sending a side for a two-day match on the 24th and the 25th. Isn't that splendid?"

"I'm not sure I can stay that long."

"But I'd hoped – No, no, I mustn't press you, I know you're busy, Nigel Palairet's told me all about it. But it would be nice if you *could* stay, because I wanted you to play in that match, and Harold's coming down from Cambridge. Specially."

"We'll have to see."

"Harold's not going to play, of course. He's just coming for the occasion. The last match. And since it will be the last match I thought I might play myself."

"Very appropriate," Hugo said.

"But that means, you see, that one place will be filled by a useless old man. Which makes it important that everyone else should be as young and as good as possible. So I'd hoped that you… But as you say, we'll have to see. We'd better get back to the cricket now. Nigel's there, and he's looking forward to seeing you."

On the field a large marquee had been erected where the pavilion used to be. At either end were flagpoles; from one of these flew the flag of Baron's Lodge, from the other the flag of the visiting side. In front of the marquee was a roped-in enclosure full of deck-chairs, from which some fifty or sixty people were watching the game, Hugo saw Nigel, who waved affectionately and then went on talking to his neighbour. The message was clear; since you've just arrived, you'll want to talk to your uncle and Georgy, won't you?

"Come inside the tent for a moment," said James. "Georgy and Bessie are arranging the tea."

Inside, the marquee was divided by a canvas partition into two unequal sections; an opening in this partition led out of the larger into the smaller, which a notice proclaimed to be the

Dressing Room. The larger, in which James and Hugo now stood, was devoted to refreshment; there were two long bars, behind one of which was a white-coated barman, a barrel of beer and many bottles of champagne, while behind the other Georgy and Bessie were busy laying out cakes and sandwiches.

"Hugo," said Georgy quietly. She came out from behind the bar and kissed him on the lips. Only Hugo knew how cold was her kiss.

"Hullo, laddie," said Bessie briefly.

"Busy now," from Georgy, "we can talk later."

"Notice anything?" said James, and pointed away from the dressing room to the far end of the tent.

There, carefully secured to the canvas wall, were the red and gold boards that Lionel had painted: the Baron's Lodge Cricket XIs over all the last thirty-five years. All but the last year, when Lionel had been dead.

"Glad I saved them," said James. "One chance to show them off if there's never another."

"They look very nice," said Hugo, trying not to remember the afternoon on which Lionel had first showed them to him.

"Think so? Good. A drink now?"

Hugo took a glass of champagne from the barman, while James, he noticed, only asked for half a pint of beer. They carried their drinks outside into the afternoon, such an afternoon as there can only be in May: blue and warm and fresh (not yet the coarse blaze of June or the languors of July); the grass still a deep green, the flags flirting with the mast heads, the birds singing of all the pleasures the coming months would bring. Pu-we. Towittawoo.

"I must circulate," James said, "you go and talk to Nigel."

A chair on one side of Nigel was empty; rather to his surprise, Hugo felt no apprehension as he took it and indeed found himself pleasantly curious to hear Nigel's news. (How are Ronnie and Mavis getting on, Nigel?) Nigel, however, proved curt rather than communicative.

"I'm glad you're here," he said. "Everything in Italy as we would wish?"

"Roughly."

"Good. We can talk of that later. I'm hoping that even with business as brisk as it is" – this with a slight nod towards his neighbour on the other side – "you'll still be able to stay through to the MCC match on the 24th and 25th."

"But I thought – "

" – I know. But it will be a great occasion, and I think – don't you, Hugo? – that both of us ought to stay for it if we possibly can."

"It won't be at all convenient."

"You must allow me to be the judge of that."

There's no choice, Hugo thought, and no point in being annoyed. After all, if every day here is as beautiful and peaceful as this one, a week at Baron's Lodge will hardly disrupt the good life. Provided that James and Georgy behave with good sense, do not start making larger claims...

"All right," he said to Nigel. "It'll probably be great fun."

"That's settled then," said Nigel. "We'll tell your uncle at tea."

And then, refusing to be drawn by Hugo's inquiry after Nancy, he began to explain, rather boringly, how Baron's Lodge had won both the matches which had been played before Hugo's arrival.

In the event, the Baron's Lodge side also scored a substantial win over the County Colts. James, delighted by this and delighted still more by the news that Hugo would definitely be staying for the MCC match, was in great form all the evening.

"Unbeaten so far," he said, "and that's how it's going to go on. Butterflies tomorrow. I think I'll play myself – get my old bones greased up for the 24th."

"Daddy, are you sure – ?" Georgiana began.

"Nonsense. Got to limber up some time."

171

After cricket was over for the day there was drink in profusion, a superb dinner which was accompanied by two wines and succeeded by port, and then brandy and whisky ad lib until midnight, James drank very moderately, though he gave no impression of conscious restraint, and indeed by eleven o'clock he was the only person among the thirty odd present who was strictly sober. Even Nigel was showing signs of exuberance. Georgy and Bessie had dined apart; and since there were no other women to hamper the conversation, it was entertaining and often indiscreet. Once again, Hugo reflected that a week at Baron's Lodge in these conditions should pass pleasantly enough. The voices buzzed and hooted and brayed round the drawing room; the french window stood open and several people had gone out on the terrace; Baron's Lodge, thought Hugo, was a little island of well ordered pleasure in a world gone mad. The place was working its old magic on him. He would have to foster his indifference with care.

He joined a little group round Nigel, who had just given a burlesque account of the "mutiny" in Santa Kytherea.

"Poor show, Nigel. Deserting the roulette wheel in the face of the enemy. Not what we expect of the Carbiniers."

"I hear they're still out there... Doing quite well now they've started..."

"...Willie Culbertson? I think his boy was here. Before James closed, of course..."

"I loved that bit about the District Commissioner's wife who wouldn't pay her losses..."

"Hugo," – it was Georgy's voice in his ear – "can you come and have a word with Bessie and me?"

Possessed by the general good humour of the hour, Hugo did not think of refusing. Only when be was outside the room did he realize that he had exchanged a warm, half-drunken jollity, amid which he might be anonymous, for the deliberate and critical regard of two women whom he detested.

"We'll go to my room," Bessie said.

"Will this take long?" asked Hugo.

"No, laddie." (It was her "You haven't washed underneath there" voice, ringing down the years.)

They climbed the stairs to Bessie's room.

"Now," Bessie said, panting slightly. "There's some whisky over there, and you can help yourself or not as you choose. Either way, Georgy and I have something to tell you, and we'll thank you to heed it."

"Just tell me what you have to say."

"This," said Georgy. "Despite everything you've done or haven't done, things have settled down quite nicely and Daddy's himself again. You're not to upset him, Hugo. You're not to spoil it all for us."

"I didn't want to come here at all. I only came because I was told Uncle James would be badly hurt if I didn't."

"You've not been slow to hurt him before," said Bessie. "But never mind that. He's happy now, and he's happy that you're here. What Georgy means is that you're not to run away again."

"You surely can't mean that I'm to stay here for good?"

"Of course not," Georgy said. "Not now. All I mean is that you must write to Daddy regularly and come to see him. Not just behave as if he didn't exist. Bessie and I don't care what you do, we never want to see you again, but because of what you mean to Daddy – God knows why – you must come here from time to time and make yourself pleasant. All we're asking, Hugo, is that you should behave decently to Daddy until he dies."

"I understand. Now you've got hold of me again, you want to involve me again."

"It's nothing very hard we're asking," Bessie said, "and it's not for ourselves."

"It makes no difference who it's for. You know very well, you must know by now, that I can't bear to be involved. But here you are, the minute I get here, spreading the net out and whining at me to wrap myself up in it again. After all the trouble I've taken to cut myself free."

"Then why," said Georgy, "have you come here? You must see that now you have come back you can't just play in a few cricket matches and then disappear."

"I came," Hugo said slowly, "to please Nigel Palairet."

"Then if you want to go on pleasing him, you'll have to go on coming here. Whatever your reasons, it comes to the same thing. And you need do so little, Hugo. Just a letter every month or so, a visit at Christmas and another to watch the County play at Canterbury in the summer. That's all."

"It would mean that I was trapped. Even if I only had to come once every ten years, I'd still be trapped."

"Then you'll just have to put up with it," Georgy said, "like anybody else. If only to please Nigel Palairet."

After he had been admonished by Georgiana and Bessie, Hugo took a walk across the cricket field. There is only this one thing, he thought, which anyone is asking of me. To be kind to James. Provided that I am kind to James, provided I don't show him what sort of person I really am, then Georgy and Bessie will be civil to me although they hate me, while Nigel will treat me, even think of me, as a friend and (far more to the point) will keep quiet about Jennifer Stevens.

Surely then it will be simpler to do what they ask? The odd letter, the occasional brief visit…what could be easier? Take this present visit, for example; it promises to be tolerable and even enjoyable. But that's just the point, he told himself; this visit is proving tolerable because James is occupied, has no time and no need to make demands of me. When I come at Christmas, the house will be empty, Lionel's ghost will be brooding over everything, Georgy and Bessie will barely be able to hide their hatred, and James will be mutely imploring me, with looks of love, to be the son that he has lost. That is what I couldn't stand, what I had to escape from; that is why I never wanted to come back – and why I must never again come back. Because if I do, I shall be choked by James' love.

He went into the marquee and struck a match to light a cigarette. The thin light lapped over the names on the boards. They were all there; his own name, Lionel's, Nigel's. He tried to remember himself as a serious little boy, setting out in white flannels and a crested cap for an afternoon's cricket. Please, sir, when am *I* going in? Please, sir, can we stop on the way home for ice cream? Please, sir... And that, of course, was how James still saw him: not even as an undergraduate, but as a little, squeaky boy, hopefully strapping on his pads. This was the illusion they were all so anxious to preserve for James – the illusion that Hugo was still innocent. It was monstrous, of course. It was against nature. This obscene little ghost in its white flannels should have been laid forever and the adult Hugo long since released. But as it was, although he had fought free from Georgy by making her hate him, he had failed to get free of James. He had nearly done so; but the old man's affection had been too tenacious and too blind, and now ill luck had brought him back again to Baron's Lodge, so that his uncle's love could only be strengthened, while any doubts (and even James must have had some) would be put to rest. Nor could he try once more to release himself, to destroy the illusion; for if he did, he himself would be destroyed by Nigel.

And so he must submit himself to James' love. He needn't come often, but come he must, and anyhow he would always be conscious that this love was lurking in wait for him, that it was there in Kent, every day and every hour, beseeching, longing, hoping. Only James' death would set him free. And yet, was this so? Surely there must be something he had overlooked? He struck another match. You gained power over your enemy, so the magicians said, by possessing his name: he would now take possession of Nigel's. He moved closer to the boards, held up the match; there it was, NHS Palairet, on three successive boards for three successive years. "NHS Palairet," he read to himself; and again; and yet again. One, two, three. Year after year... *But of course.* How could he have missed it? Time.

Time. Not the time it would take for James to die, but just a few weeks, a few days even. Because, however valid was the evidence which Nigel claimed to possess, *he must either use it soon or not at all*. If he used it, he must explain how and when he came by it – and they would certainly check on his movements, so he could not falsify the dates. And if he did not use it at once, or nearly so, they would want to know why he had concealed it, why he had been silent when he knew, or suspected, the truth about the crime. Nigel must act before the end of May (at the very outside) or he could never act – unless he wished to accuse himself of being an accessory after a murder. His threat held good for just about as long as the cricket week would last (no doubt he could scrape up reasons for having delayed until then), but after that it would be impossible to implement and therefore useless. After the MCC match, he, Hugo, would be free to go away for good and never again be seen or heard of at Baron's Lodge.

But even as he congratulated himself his elation ebbed. For the point was so simple that Nigel could not have overlooked it. Nigel had used his knowledge to bring Hugo to Baron's Lodge and then to make him consent to stay for the final match. But he must know that stuff so delicate as this knowledge could never keep, that if he did not use it within another week or so he never could, and that after that time Hugo would be free of him. And since he must know all this, he could not be without a further plan. If Nigel undertook a thing, he saw it through; he had undertaken to keep James happy, and he would go on keeping him happy – for as long as James lived and not just until the stumps were drawn for the last time at Baron's Lodge. So what did Nigel intend to do? The simplest way of finding out was to ask him. If he had an infallible plan, then he would answer straight out, for there would be no point in concealment. If, on the other hand, his scheme depended on trickery or bluff, then whatever the answer he gave, it might well present Hugo with some sort of clue. Either way, there was everything to be said for inquiry and nothing at all against it. With care and concentration, Hugo stubbed his cigarette once into the initial "P" of all three Palairets and started back to join the party. Tomorrow he would get Nigel to himself and put the question.

Since James himself was playing in the match against the Butterflies, he was leading the Baron's Lodge side. Having won the toss he chose to bat. Hugo and Nigel, who were both playing, were down to bat respectively at number six and number nine.

"It would be a great help," said Hugo to Nigel, "if you would give me a ball or two at the nets. I haven't played a stroke since last June."

They left the ground, walked past the swimming pool (which was being filled in case any of James' guests fancied a bathe), through a rose garden, and on to a smooth and sizeable lawn which was known as Truepenny and on which practice nets had been put up. After Nigel had sent him down some five or six balls, all of which he played correctly and neatly, Hugo opened his shoulders and hit the next one hard and high over Nigel's head in the direction of a thick shrubbery.

"Sorry about that," he said, "forgot myself."

"Let's have a look for it," Nigel said.

They walked towards the shrubbery. A distant burst of clapping from the field indicated that the match had now begun, while two hundred yards in the other direction a maid was shaking a small carpet from a window in the house. Hugo thrust with his bat at a lavender bush.

"It doesn't matter," he said. "It was only an old one."

"Just a quick look…"

"Nigel," said Hugo, leaning on his bat. "What are you going to do after the cricket is over?"

"Go back to London. I really ought to be there now. Nancy's been alone too much."

"But what are you going to do about me?"

"About you?" said Nigel slowly.

"Yes. You've taken great trouble to get me here. Presumably you won't want to let me go. You'll want me to go on seeing my uncle?"

"I rather hoped that you too would want that. I thought that when you saw the place again, saw how happy your uncle was to see you, you'd be glad to come back from time to time. Or at least that you'd be shamed into it."

"You know me better than that, Nigel. I grant you it's quite pleasant here just now – blue skies and lots of people and plenty of cricket to keep everyone busy. But it won't always be like this. And even if it were, I still wouldn't come, and you know very well why not."

"Because you are afraid of a good man's love."

"Because I hate his love. Unless you've got some way of forcing me. I shan't come back here again."

"You know that you must pay my price if you want my silence," Nigel said.

"I also know that if you keep silence much longer you'll have to keep it for good."

Nigel smiled.

"You're quite right," he said. "I've been thinking about that."

"And what have you decided?"

Nigel stooped to push aside a small clump of gorse and picked up a cricket ball.

"This isn't the one we were using," he said.

"They're always getting lost in here. There must be hundreds... What have you decided, Nigel?"

"Nothing. I'm going to let Nancy decide."

"*Nancy?*"

"Yes. Nancy's the expert on you, Hugo. She always knew what you were up to, but she let you get away with it because she wanted you in bed. She bears you no hard feelings, but she's quite ready to help me tie you down. She regards it as an interesting problem – no more and no less. I've no doubt she'll come up with a solution."

"But she hasn't yet?" said Hugo.

"I'll let you know when she does," said Nigel. "There's plenty of time. Would you like a few more balls? Or shall we go back and watch?"

When Hugo went in to bat, the Baron's Lodge side had lost four wickets for seventy runs.

"Not good enough," said James. "Take your time, dear boy."

At first Hugo took it. Playing with care and mostly off the back foot, he scored only twenty-five runs during his first hour at the crease. But towards lunch-time, as the bowlers began to tire, he became more adventurous. Twice running he cut the ball very late through the slips for four; the next over, he slashed the ball square through the covers to the boundary (a brilliant, beautiful, and very dangerous stroke), and then hit it over the bowler's head and into the enclosure for six. A few minutes later he completed his fifty with a huge pull shot (the same that had killed Lionel) which sent the ball clean out of the ground and into the swimming pool. At lunch-time Baron's Lodge had scored one hundred and sixty for seven wickets and Hugo, who had now been joined by Nigel, had made seventy-one not out.

James was crimson with pleasure and pride.

"Just what was needed, dear boy," he burbled, handing Hugo a quart tankard of beer. "Wait till they weaken, then wallop them. If you and Nigel can get another quick fifty after lunch, we'll be dead set."

In the event, Hugo and Nigel put on eighty more runs in forty minutes. Nigel was a vigorous player who hit with natural grace off the front foot and was suited by the quick wicket. He gathered thirty-five from drives and sweeps, while Hugo improved, if anything, on his pre-lunch versatility and reached his century with a leg glance for four which he played from well outside the off stump. A few balls later Nigel was caught at the wicket and Hugo was joined by James.

"Twenty minutes with the throttle full out, dear boy, and then we'll declare."

Most of the bowling went to Hugo; but such balls as James received he played with a delicacy which recalled and honoured the County batsman of the 'twenties. By the time he declared the innings closed, James had scored a stylish fifteen, mostly in singles, and Hugo had made thirty more, eighteen of them in sixes.

"You ought to have gone in earlier," Hugo found himself saying. "I'd forgotten what a pleasure it is to watch you bat."

"Think so, dear boy?" said James, modest and happy. "Must admit, I enjoyed myself. Batting opposite you...it made me feel good, very good."

But as James turned his eyes towards him, Hugo made off quickly to the dressing-room.

Baron's Lodge bowled out the Butterflies with eight runs and two minutes to spare. It had been, everyone was agreed, a great match – which would now be fitly celebrated, as most of the Butterflies had accepted an invitation to stay to dinner.

This was even more sumptuous than it had been on the previous evening. Uncle James must be spending hundreds, Hugo thought. But then, it's his last fling. This time next year the field will be covered with nasty little houses, the once elegant scene disgraced by greasy caps and varicose veins, by the shrill, smelly offspring of the poor. Necessity's revenge on style. Mrs Hunt's revenge on a pride and quality which she had not understood. Hugo Warren's revenge (for it also came to that) on those who had been too kind.

For himself, thought Hugo, he could not see the school go without a certain regret. Once leave aside his personal reasons for wishing to be rid of it all, then he had to admit that in Baron's Lodge there could be and had been an admissible version of the good life. Narrow and at odds with the age, complacent and often snobbish, the doctrine of Baron's Lodge was not without dignity and truth. His uncle had provided a good grounding in the classical tongues, on which most of the language and literature of Europe depended, he had taught those who wished to learn how to play the most intricate and beautiful of all games, and he had dealt tolerantly and decently with the men and boys in his charge. There was a lot to be said for this (as far as it went) and it was a pity it must all be at an end.

The fact remained that it was at an end. Nothing, he had told Jennifer, is more paralysing then regret; he himself must not fall victim now. Baron's Lodge, the school, was a thing of the past; his problem was Baron's Lodge the home, the home with its ties and claims which others were so determined to press on him. First Nigel had compelled him to recognize them; and now, it seemed, the office was being transferred to Nancy. But why should he be afraid of Nancy? What could she think up that Nigel couldn't – this poor woman with her shivers and shouts of lust, who had been so obsessed with his embraces that she had allowed him to steal her husband's fortune? What could Nancy do? Nothing, his reason told him, nothing at all. But he remembered the cool figure that had stood beside Nigel on the Acropolis, so grim and formidable until she had smiled; he remembered the efficient woman of business who had shown neither scruple nor weakness in months save only when naked under his own caress; and he had a sudden vision of Nancy, fully clothed and unsmiling, her fingers curved into claws, rising from a disarrayed bed in Chester Row like a vampire from the grave.

After the Butterfly dinner, Nigel slipped away to a telephone box to ring up Nancy. Having established that everything in Chester Row was in good order, he raised the subject of Hugo.

"He's behaving well enough," he told Nancy briefly. "But when he goes he's going for good."

"And you're still determined this mustn't happen?"

"Yes. I've been to too much trouble in all this to see it wasted now."

"Very well," said Nancy. "I've thought about this for a long time, and here is what you must do…"

For some minutes Nigel listened as Nancy gave precise and lucid instructions. Then, with a sigh, he replaced the receiver and walked back through the pale blue evening to Baron's Lodge.

XV

When harold arrived the evening before the MCC match, he learnt that the Baron's Lodge team had so far won all its matches but two, both of these having been honourably drawn. James, who was particularly anxious that this unbeaten record should be maintained, was in a state of feverish excitement about the next day. At one point he had even spoken of not playing himself, in order to "make room for young blood"; but he had been persuaded that it was proper and even mandatory that he himself should lead the side on this, the last match of all.

"Quite right," said Harold. "And anyhow they tell me you've been in good form."

"Not too bad for an old man," said James with modest pleasure. "Fifteen not out against the Butterflies and twenty-two yesterday against some very decent Forester bowling."

"So of course you must play," said Harold; and then, leaving James deep in thought about the batting order, he went to look for Georgy.

"How's Hugo been behaving?" he said at once.

"Rather well. A bit distant, but nothing you could object to."

"And will he go on coming to see your father?"

"I don't know," said Georgy. "He refused at first, then said he would because of Nigel Palairet. It could mean anything. I no longer understand him, you see. He's become...alien."

"Perhaps he always was."

Then Harold went to find Hugo.

"What do you think of your uncle?" Harold said.

"He seems very well."

"You know why. All this cricket, and all his friends, and, not least, seeing you again. After this match, he'll be feeling rather flat. I suppose you wouldn't think of staying on for a day or two?"

"No."

"But I thought you'd promised Georgy – "

"I've changed my mind. Because all the reward I've had for coming at all is to have people nagging at me like you're doing now."

"Your trouble," said Harold, "is that you're a second rate man with certain minor capacities which you're too proud to settle for. You're too proud to do the little things you *could* do. You could have been a good schoolmaster, in a modest way, and a great help to James. Even now, you could give him a lot of happiness. But no, not you. You're too grand, too greedy, for such simple things. You must for ever be trying to catch up with some new and more inflated idea of your own importance."

"I haven't done too badly, Harold. I've become quite rich, you know. I lead a pleasant and civilized life. I read books. I look at things. I think."

"While you're being so smug about it all, perhaps you'd care to tell me where the money came from."

"You might say," said Hugo, "that I did a lucky piece of business."

"I might say that you're a bloody little crook."

"Don't start trouble, Harold. For the moment at least everyone is happy here. You wouldn't want to spoil it?"

Harold grunted and stumped off, but for the rest of the evening he made himself agreeable to everybody, Hugo included. Not that he had to suffer Hugo for long. Although the refreshments were as lavish as ever, James, apologetic but firm, insisted that those who were to play in next day's match should be in bed by ten-thirty sharp. With James and Hugo out of the way, Harold approached Nigel (whom James had pronounced, with regret, to be too light-weight a player for so serious an occasion) and came straight to the point.

"Whatever it is you do in Chester Row," he said, "Hugo had evidently reaped considerable benefit. He must be grateful to you."

"I doubt it," Nigel said. "Gratitude is not his *forte*."

"But you must have *some* influence with him."

"Perhaps."

"Then get him to stay here after the cricket's over. Or at least to promise to come again very soon."

"I see," Nigel smiled coolly. "You too want to spare James Escome the truth about his precious nephew."

"I'm an old friend of Lionel's, of them all."

"You don't need to explain. I'm on your side."

"Well then?"

"Hugo," said Nigel, "is determined to push off again for good. He is not in the mood to listen to polite requests."

"So I've found out. It seems he was more docile with Georgiana and Bessie, though. He said he'd do what they asked, because of you. Why was that?"

"At that time he thought I had a hold over him. So I had, but it gets weaker every day. It follows that we must arrange something else. Perhaps you would care to assist me in this? I need someone with a logical and strictly objective turn of mind. I don't know you, of course, but I've read some of your books – "

" – Which?" said Harold, flattered.

"One on the pre-Socratics and another on primitive notions of godhead – a subject that particularly interests me. It seems to me that you may have the qualities needed. Bessie and Georgiana think so too."

"Qualities needed for what?"

"For what is to be done. Let us go outside," said Nigel, moving towards the french window, "and get a little privacy and fresh air. First of all, you'd better hear exactly what our young friend has been up to since he left London…"

The MCC had gathered a side of amateurs, most of whom had played for County Second XIs at one time or another and three of whom had played full seasons in first class cricket, albeit some years ago. This was opposition of a calibre unlike anything yet seen during James' cricket week; there would be no room for error or laxity, as was plainly apparent from the very beginning of the match. The MCC, having won the toss and chosen to bat, sent in two grizzled left-handers, the more grizzled of whom, receiving as his first ball a high and fast full toss, hit it calmly over square leg and out of the ground, thus removing most of its shine and much of the bowler's self-esteem. There followed another full toss and two long hops, each of which was dispatched, with an efficiency so spare as to be almost casual, for four runs. After this the play settled down a bit, but no one was left in any doubt how matters stood: the opposition was a tough and old-fashioned bunch of campaigners who would hit bad balls, stop good ones, and drop dead on the ground sooner than give away one run in a hundred.

By lunch time, the MCC had made a hundred and ninety runs for the loss of two wickets. Since this was to be a two day match, there was no prospect of an early declaration, and the Baron's Lodge contingent faced a grim afternoon ahead. The only one who was quite undaunted was James, who remarked that three lucky balls, which could happen at any moment, would be quite enough to restore the balance. After lunch, in the hope of illustrating this principle, he tried a number of quick changes in the bowling; but the MCC batsmen had been in the game too long to be caught out by this kind of trick, and the only wicket to fall before three o'clock went to a grotesque leg break bowled by James himself – a ball which seemed to come back almost square behind the batsman's legs to hit his stumps. This made the score two hundred and seventy for three.

There followed another hour and a half of vigorous and unsparing batting, until at teatime, with three hundred and ninety runs on the board, the MCC declared.

The first innings of Baron's Lodge opened with a series of disasters. The first batsman fell inside five minutes to a vicious yorker; number three was out to the very next ball, which went away from him at the last moment, touching the edge of the bat (if he hadn't been a very good player he would have missed it altogether) and proceeding straight into the wicket-keeper's gloves with a dull plop; and two overs later number four called an eccentric run to cover point and was run out by six foot clear. Nor did matters mend when Hugo went in; having driven a couple of balls to the long off boundary and being apparently well set, he received the only shooter of the entire week (all the wickets had been immaculately prepared) and looked round to see the three stumps forming a perfect equilateral triangle on the ground. His scowl was visible from the marquee; and Bessie, who was taking a moment off from clearing up the tea things, laughed so loudly that several MCC men in the field raised their eyebrows, the only facial movement they made during the entire day except to consume food and drink.

After this, however, with a score of only thirty runs for four wickets, Baron's Lodge began to settle down. Number two, a dull but extremely sound player, looked as if he were capable of staying there for life, and number six, who now joined him, was blessed with that quality against which even the dour authority of the MCC must be powerless: he was in luck. He snicked his first ball through the slips for four, chopped the second between his legs for two, and then, having sent short leg the kind of catch one gives a five-year old child at a picnic, saw it slide like soap through the unfortunate man's hands and drop to the ground with the deliberation of a freshly ejected cow-pat. This mistake cost the fielding side dear; for despite his erratic start, number six was a correct and cool-headed player, just the man for an emergency, and he now proceeded to play the bowling with an unhurried, almost intellectual competence which the MCC players themselves could hardly have improved upon. The score went steadily up, from forty to sixty, from sixty to a hundred; and when stumps were drawn at half past six Baron's Lodge had made a hundred and fifty odd for five wickets (number two having played so far back to a ball that he had hit his own stumps). As James remarked, Baron's Lodge was by no means out of danger but was very definitely still in the match.

Partly because of the dedicated nature of the MCC players, partly because this was the last night but one of the cricket week (the last night on which people could still look forward) dinner was a rather muted affair, more formal than usual and far less gay. Although the match was still a live concern, there was an air of anti-climax, almost of futility, to which most people responded by going early to bed. James, solicitous for the health of his team, was not displeased by this ("When we've won the match we can have a real booze-up"), but when he himself said good night he urged all the non-players to stay and drink as late as they wished.

"There are not many nights left," he said wistfully, and waved his hand from the doorway in what might almost have been a total valediction.

"Now," said Nigel to Harold when the old man had gone, "you're absolutely clear about tomorrow?"

"Yes," said Harold indifferently.

"No doubts?"

"After what you told me last night," said Harold, "it is too late for doubts."

The next morning saw Baron's Lodge battling hard but on the whole successfully to make up ground. Number six continued to cash in on his early good luck with controlled and accurate batting; and by the time the seventh wicket had fallen and he was joined by James, the score had advanced to two hundred and forty. Another hundred runs, and Baron's Lodge would be out of trouble.

James had acquitted himself very decently when playing in earlier matches, but he was now up against a standard of bowling which he had not faced for many years. At first he seemed confused and alarmed; his strokes were played without heart and even without hope, scrappy, aimless strokes, bearing little relation to the balls bowled, like those of a sulky schoolboy who has been forced to play against his will. Then, when the spectators were beginning to feel sad and embarrassed for him, he received a fast, short ball outside the off stump. In the old days this had been his favourite of all things; and even now some reflex stirred from its long sleep and took him into action: over came his left foot, up and across went the bat, all wrist and balance, quick and inevitable as a striking snake, and almost before the shot was completed the ball had flashed past cover and was at the boundary. It was the classical square cut off the front foot, a stroke which had been old-fashioned even when it delighted the Kentish crowds in the 'twenties and which had not been seen in cricket of any consequence since the old Nawab of Pataudi died. It was so unexpected, so beautiful, so absolute in its kind, that for a moment there was complete silence. Then, for the first time since the match started, the MCC players began to clap. Gravely and slowly, without exaggeration but without stint, they applauded what each of them recognized as the work of a master hand.

And now it was for James as if all the years had fallen away and he was back on the Canterbury green in the full pride of his youth and skill. There was no more fumbling and snatching, no more dithering and backing away. Now that he had played his square cut everything was come right. Each stroke was as sure as the one before, neat, essential and precise. Most of them, to be sure, were strokes which scored behind the wicket or not at all (for where should an old man find strength to drive and force?), but they were crisp and firm, models of seemliness and grace. He cut square, he cut late; he glanced the ball to leg off the back foot and off the front; he played back in defence with the calculated suavity of a matador; when he hooked, it was with a feather-light touch, a mere deflection, by which he stole for his own end the bowler's power. It was a captain's innings in time of need; he batted from a quarter past twelve to half past one; and when he came back to the marquee, having declared the Baron's Lodge innings closed for 401 runs of which he himself had made sixty-five, the spectators rose to greet him with a great shout of triumph, many of them turning away to hide the tears which were running down their cheeks.

"Circumstances quite helpful so far," said Nigel to Harold during the lunch interval.

"I suppose so," answered Harold, and went on eating his cold salmon with prudence and solemnity.

The MCC batted from after lunch until tea at four forty-five. Swiftly and dispassionately, they made three hundred and thirty-two runs for the loss of seven wickets. By declaring when they did, they left Baron's Lodge with three hundred and twenty-two runs to make in two hours (between five and seven, for either captain could ask for an extra half-hour after six-thirty). It was, on the whole, a sporting declaration; it left Baron's Lodge with an outside but, given the state of the ground, quite feasible chance. Even so, many captains would have ordered their men to play out time for a draw. Not James. "All or nothing," he said as he led his side off the field. "Never mind the wickets. We want *runs*."

"Remember," said Nigel to Harold during the tea interval, "as soon as the umpires pull the stumps."

In order to save time, James posted members and supporters of the Baron's Lodge side all round the field so that they might gather the ball the moment it reached the boundary and return it to the bowler. For the first quarter of an hour of the Baron's Lodge innings this precaution was otiose. True, the opening batsman hit a six off his second ball; but he was clean bowled by the ball which followed it, and numbers three and four fared much the same. Number two survived, but he had neither the temperament nor the aptitude for aggressive play; so that when Hugo came in at number five, with the score at twenty for three, it was up to him to take charge without delay.

His behaviour was cool and assured. The first three balls he received he treated with modest deference (time spent in reconnaissance is *never* wasted). The fourth ball, which was only just short of a length, he hooked nippily for four, and the fifth, which was well up to him and the last of the over, he pushed away towards mid-wicket for a single. Then, facing the bowling at the other end, he once again played three cautious exploratory shots – only to follow them with two rangy drives through the covers and another quick single to mid-wicket off the last ball of the over.

It had been a long day, and tough as the MCC bowlers were, they were beginning to fail in speed and accuracy. For some overs, Hugo cut, hooked and drove with evident ease; then, when the MCC tried the sensible but obvious tactic of putting on slow spin bowlers to tempt him into indiscriminate hitting, he kept his head, refrained from trying to strike the ball half-volley, and scored a quick succession of twos and singles either off the back foot or by leaving his ground and playing the ball carefully yet firmly before it pitched. But although the runs were coming very nicely, the rate of scoring at five-thirty (sixty-seven runs in the first half-hour) was still not quite high enough to bring the Baron's Lodge total to three hundred and twenty-two by seven o'clock.

At this stage number two, desperate to pay his way, played a pull shot of almost blasphemous ineptness and was succeeded by number six, who was very much more suited to play the kind of innings required. For ten minutes all went well; but at five forty-five number six, wrought upon by the perennial temptation to hit a leg break at the half volley, mistimed his stroke and was caught by long off. Number seven and number eight both scored a few useful runs, but both got overexcited and before long picked the wrong balls to hit. When James joined Hugo at the wicket the time was ten minutes past six and the score was a hundred and seventy; if Baron's Lodge were to win now, they must score at the rate of three runs a minute.

"You can rely on me to stay here, dear boy," said James, "but you'll have to get the runs."

It was now that Hugo started to put on real pressure. The ground, though of ample size for little boys, was rather on the small side for grown men. It followed that lofted shots, in time of emergency, were often good investments: even if improperly hit, they were liable to sag over the boundary line, immune from being caught, for unmerited sixes. From now on, therefore, and whenever possible, Hugo started to lift the ball. This policy was rewarded by five sixes (two of them at least rather gungy ones) in three overs, quite apart from the runs he scored along the ground. Every time the ball reached the boundary, it was instantly retrieved and returned by one of the onlookers stationed for the purpose; and by half past six the score had reached two hundred and thirty-eight

James' part was unspectacular but demanding. Every time he was left with the bowling, he had to contrive to place the ball for a single so that Hugo might renew his efforts. It was a measure of his cunning that only twice in his first half-hour at the crease did he receive two consecutive balls and that not once did he receive more than two. Hugo, in a foam of sweat, his face glowing red as a winter's sun, continued game; but he was flagging a little now and badly needed the respite which James could not give him.

"One last effort, dear boy," James called up the pitch between the overs. "One last effort…"

For now the shadows were lengthening over the ground and the birds were failing in their song. There were forty runs to be got and twenty minutes in which to get them. The MCC captain, knowing that Hugo must soon make a mistake if only from weariness, was continuing with the slow bowlers who were the more likely to elicit it. One last effort, thought Hugo; now or never. He faced up to a tall, stringy, left-handed bowler, who was giving the ball plenty of air and bringing it in, with pungency, from the leg. One last effort.

The first ball of the over was slightly overpitched and outside the off-stump. Left elbow well up, left foot well across, Hugo drove it into the air over extra cover's head and saw it land just over the boundary line. The next ball was also on the off, but shorter and quicker: this time he put his right foot across and cut it just backward of square; third man, running round the boundary, saved the four, but Hugo and James ran a comfortable two. That's eight of them, Hugo thought. As the bowler's arm came over for the third time, Hugo saw him cock his wrist to turn the ball, for a change, from the off. I'll teach him to bowl Chinamen, Hugo thought; *hit with the spin*. He smashed into the ball with a rancorous cross bat and for the second time that week holed out in the swimming pool. For the fourth ball of the over, the bowler adopted a precisely similar action – wrist cocked for the Chinaman that would come in from the off. But he's faking, Hugo thought; it's going to be a googly, it's going to come in from the leg, and if it's that much higher in the air I'll be certain. It was that much higher. Back over his head then, no time for refinements now, back over his head hard and high. Hugo jumped out of his crease, did not quite get his foot to the ball, and hit it ballooning into the air with a good deal of slice. On the boundary long off waited, shading his eyes with his hands; but Hugo's luck held, and what would have been a catch on seven grounds out of ten cleared the boundary by five yards. The fifth ball was well short on the leg side; his arms felt like lead, but he managed to scrabble it away for two. The sixth ball was straight and quickish; abandoning all thought, Hugo just swished; he caught the ball on the meat, and it sizzled away crutch high between the bowler and mid-on to the boundary. He had scored twenty-six runs in the one over, and he was utterly spent.

"That's it dear boy," called James as the fieldsmen crossed over. "There's time for me to get the rest."

This he now did, crisply and prettily, and had the honour, some five minutes before the time for close of play. Moving from the wicket half dazed with triumph and fatigue, neither he nor Hugo saw Harold, who, as the umpires pulled up the stumps, walked rapidly away towards the house.

In the marquee all was laughter, confusion and champagne. Nigel managed to draw Hugo aside for a moment and said, "You're still leaving tomorrow?"

"Yes," said Hugo.

"And you won't come back?"

"No."

"You're sure, Hugo? This is your last chance."

"Of course I'm sure. And what do you mean, my last chance?"

"You'll find out very soon."

Hugo shrugged and returned to the drinkers. Congratulations poured round him; James was grinning like an imbecile and drinking glass after glass of champagne; the MCC players were murmuring a discreet appraisal of the two days' play. Then Hugo began to feel unwell; he felt the vomit beginning to rise, the ground moving under his feet. Nigel appeared beside him.

"I put something in your drink," Nigel whispered. "You'd better come outside."

Unable to help himself, Hugo mumbled an excuse to those nearest him and followed Nigel out of the tent.

"This way," Nigel said.

He led off across the field, Hugo stumbling at his side and retching out little bursts of vomit. They rounded a hedge, went down a short path, and there in front of them was the swimming pool. Harold was standing beside it, as were Georgiana and Bessie.

"Take off his blazer and boots," Nigel said, and pushed Hugo down on a bench.

Bessie came forward, unbuttoned and removed Hugo's blazer, unlaced and pulled off his boots, Hugo sat absolutely still save when he jerked his head forward to vomit.

"It wasn't really surprising," said Nigel, "that the sun and the excitement and the exertion and the drink on top of everything else should have made you feel rather light headed. And what more natural than that you should have fancied a bathe to cool yourself off? Such at least was the intention you confided to me at the tent. I agreed to come with you, not to swim because I *can't* swim, Hugo, but to bear you company. And in you went naked, just as you used to when you were here as a boy, because James has always discouraged prudishness in the young. Strip him," he said, turning to Bessie and Georgy.

Bessie and Georgy moved forward. Georgy took off his socks Bessie his shirt. Hugo sat quite still. Slowly and carefully, Georgy unbuttoned his fly, then Bessie eased him down until he was half lying on the bench. While Bessie supported his buttocks, Georgy began to tug at the bottom of his trousers; soon they were halfway down his thighs, then round his ankles, then completely off. Nigel heaved him to his feet and sent him spinning into the pool.

"What we both unluckily forgot," Nigel went on, "is that people who bathe in cold water after an intense physical effort are liable to suffer from cramp."

Hugo floundered in the water. He could not use his arms and legs, he could not keep his head up, he felt himself sinking, gradually but inevitably, down into unfathomable deeps. After all, he thought through the buzzing and humming in his brain, perhaps this is what I always really wanted; to find freedom from being involved.

"Anyway," he heard Nigel saying from a thousand miles away, "it looked like cramp to me. I jumped in to help you, but you were in the deep end and I couldn't reach you."

He jumped into the shallow end, shoes and all, and waded forward.

"And when Harold appeared with Georgy and Bessie, all of them thought it must be cramp too. 'I can't swim, I can't help him,' I called to Harold, and almost at once he dived in…"

Harold loosened his tie, took off his jacket and shoes, and dived into the water. I hope he's not going to save me, Hugo thought; it's much better like this, so warm and soft…

"At first it seemed that Harold would get there in time…"

Harold took a few tentative strokes across the bath. "…However," intoned Nigel, "just as Harold reached you, you went under once more. And then, when Harold finally got you out, although Bessie went to work with artificial respiration, it turned out to be too late. She forced a lot of water and champagne out of you, but it was too late."

What was the good life, Hugo thought, but a kind of sleep. For the last time he sank away from the air.

"And of course everyone, especially your uncle, was very sad. But you see, Hugo," Nigel murmured on, "he had such splendid memories of you. Had you lived, you would only have deserted and disappointed him. But as it was, once he got over his grief, he could console himself with thinking of you as you were when you died your untimely death. You had become a fixed image – for ever young, triumphant, and loyal, in all appearance, to himself. Unchangeably beautiful because you were dead. And even when the wretched little council houses went up on his cricket ground, James Escome could always remember the last, wonderful match, in which he and his beloved nephew, against all the odds, had carried the day for Baron's Lodge."

Deal
June 15th, 1962

SIMON RAVEN

MORNING STAR

This first volume in Simon Raven's *First-Born of Egypt* saga opens with the christening of the Marquess Canteloupe's son and heir, Sarum of Old Sarum. The ceremony, attended by the godparents and the real father, Fielding Gray, is not without drama.

The christening introduces a bizarre cast of eccentric characters and complicated relationships. In *Morning Star* we meet the brilliant but troublesome teenager Marius Stern. Marius' increasingly outrageous behaviour has him constantly on the verge of expulsion from prep school. When his parents are kidnapped, apparently without reason, events take a turn for the worse.

THE FACE OF THE WATERS

This is the second volume of Simon Raven's *First-Born of Egypt* series. Marius Stern, the wayward son of Gregory Stern, has survived earlier escapades and is safely back at prep school – assisted by his father's generous contribution to the school's new shooting-range. Fielding Gray and Jeremy Morrison are returning home via Venice, where they encounter the friar, Piero, an ex-male whore and a figure from a shared but distant past.

Back in England, at the Wiltshire family home, Lord Canteloupe is restless. He finds his calm disturbed by events: the arrival of Piero; Jeremy's father's threat to saddle his son with the responsibility of the family estate; and the dramatic resistance of Gregory Stern to attempted blackmail.

SIMON RAVEN

BEFORE THE COCK CROW

This is the third volume in Simon Raven's *First-Born of Egypt* saga. The story opens with Lord Canteloupe's strange toast to 'absent friends'. His wife Baby has recently died and Canteloupe has been left her retarded son, Lord Sarum of Old Sarum. This child is not his, but has been conceived by Major Fielding Gray. In Italy there is an illegitimate child with a legitimate claim to the estate, whom Canteloupe wants silenced.

NEW SEED FOR OLD

The fourth in the *First-Born of Egypt* series has Lord Canteloupe wanting a satisfactory heir so that his dynasty may continue. Unfortunately, Lord Canteloupe is impotent and his existing heir, little Tully Sarum, is not of sound mind.

His wife Theodosia is prepared to do her duty when a suitable partner is found. Finding the man and the occasion proves somewhat tricky however, and it is not until Lord Canteloupe goes up to Lord's for the first match of the season that progress is made.

SIMON RAVEN

BLOOD OF MY BONE

In this fifth volume of Simon Raven's *First-Born of Egypt* series, the death of the Provost of a large school is a catalyst for a series of disgraceful doings in the continuing saga of the Canteloupes and their circle.

Marius, under-age father of the new Lady Canteloupe's dutifully produced heir to the family estate, is warned against the malign influence of Raisley Conyngham. Classics teacher at his school, Conyngham is well aware of the sway he has over Marius, who has already revealed himself a keen student of 'the refinements of hell'. With fate intervening, the stage is set for another deliciously wicked instalment.

IN THE IMAGE OF GOD

The sixth in the *First-Born of Egypt* series sees Raisley Conyngham, Classics teacher at a large school, exert a powerful influence over Marius Stern. His young pupil, however, is no defenceless victim.

Marius has a ruthless streak and an ability to sidestep tests and traps that are laid for him. Which is just as well because everybody is after something from him…

OTHER TITLES BY SIMON RAVEN AVAILABLE DIRECT
FROM HOUSE OF STRATUS

Quantity		£	$(US)	$(CAN)	€
☐	BEFORE THE COCK CROW	7.99	12.99	17.49	13.00
☐	BIRD OF ILL OMEN	7.99	12.99	17.49	13.00
☐	BLOOD OF MY BONE	7.99	12.99	17.49	13.00
☐	BROTHER CAIN	7.99	12.99	17.49	13.00
☐	DOCTORS WEAR SCARLET	7.99	12.99	17.49	13.00
☐	THE FACE OF THE WATERS	7.99	12.99	17.49	13.00
☐	THE FORTUNES OF FINGEL	7.99	12.99	17.49	13.00
☐	IN THE IMAGE OF GOD	7.99	12.99	17.49	13.00
☐	AN INCH OF FORTUNE	7.99	12.99	17.49	13.00
☐	MORNING STAR	7.99	12.99	17.49	13.00
☐	NEW SEED FOR OLD	7.99	12.99	17.49	13.00
☐	THE ROSES OF PICARDIE	7.99	12.99	17.49	13.00
☐	SEPTEMBER CASTLE	7.99	12.99	17.49	13.00
☐	SHADOWS ON THE GRASS	7.99	12.99	17.49	13.00
☐	THE TROUBADOUR	7.99	12.99	17.49	13.00

ALL HOUSE OF STRATUS BOOKS ARE AVAILABLE FROM GOOD BOOKSHOPS
OR DIRECT FROM THE PUBLISHER:

Internet: **www.houseofstratus.com** including author interviews, reviews, features.

Email: **sales@houseofstratus.com** please quote author, title and credit card details.

Hotline: UK ONLY: **0800 169 1780**, please quote author, title and credit card details.
INTERNATIONAL: **+44 (0) 20 7494 6400**, please quote author, title and credit card details.

Send to: **House of Stratus Sales Department**
24c Old Burlington Street
London
W1X 1RL
UK

Please allow for postage costs charged per order plus an amount per book as set out in the tables below:

	£(Sterling)	$(US)	$(CAN)	€(Euros)
Cost per order				
UK	2.00	3.00	4.50	3.30
Europe	3.00	4.50	6.75	5.00
North America	3.00	4.50	6.75	5.00
Rest of World	3.00	4.50	6.75	5.00
Additional cost per book				
UK	0.50	0.75	1.15	0.85
Europe	1.00	1.50	2.30	1.70
North America	2.00	3.00	4.60	3.40
Rest of World	2.50	3.75	5.75	4.25

PLEASE SEND CHEQUE, POSTAL ORDER (STERLING ONLY), EUROCHEQUE, OR INTERNATIONAL MONEY ORDER (PLEASE CIRCLE METHOD OF PAYMENT YOU WISH TO USE)
MAKE PAYABLE TO: STRATUS HOLDINGS plc

Cost of book(s): —————————— Example: 3 x books at £6.99 each: £20.97

Cost of order: —————————— Example: £2.00 (Delivery to UK address)

Additional cost per book: —————— Example: 3 x £0.50: £1.50

Order total including postage: ——— Example: £24.47

Please tick currency you wish to use and add total amount of order:

☐ £ (Sterling)   ☐ $ (US)   ☐ $ (CAN)   ☐ € (EUROS)

VISA, MASTERCARD, SWITCH, AMEX, SOLO, JCB:

☐ ☐ ☐ ☐ ☐ ☐ ☐ ☐ ☐ ☐ ☐ ☐ ☐ ☐ ☐ ☐ ☐ ☐ ☐ ☐

Issue number (Switch only):

☐ ☐ ☐

Start Date: **Expiry Date:**

☐ ☐ / ☐ ☐   ☐ ☐ / ☐ ☐

Signature: ————————————

NAME: ————————————————————

ADDRESS: ————————————————————

————————————————————

POSTCODE: —————————

Please allow 28 days for delivery.

Prices subject to change without notice.
Please tick box if you do not wish to receive any additional information. ☐

House of Stratus publishes many other titles in this genre; please check our website (**www.houseofstratus.com**) for more details.